ONE LESS SCANDALOUS EARL

BLUESTOCKINGS DEFYING ROGUES BOOK SIX

DAWN BROWER

MONARCHAL GLENN PRESS

ONE LESS SCANDALOUS EARL

"Being deeply loved by someone gives you strength, while loving someone deeply gives you courage."

— LAO TZU

ACKNOWLEDGMENTS

Thanks to those that helped me polish this book. Elizabeth you're my number one. You're the best ever. Also thanks once again to my awesome editor, Victoria Miller. You make me a better writer and without you I might not be where I am today.

This book is for all the readers that have been waiting for Shelby's story. I hope it meets all of your expectations.

CHAPTER 1

London 1824

*I*t was a warm afternoon for late spring. Summer was around the corner, and most of the aristocracy would retreat to their country estates. Something Lady Kaitlin Evans wished was an option for her. She resided with her uncle, the Earl of Coventry, and he preferred town life. He rarely retired to his country estate. With her brother, Collin, still away at school and her cousin, Marian, married less than a year ago—Kaitlin was lonely.

She was happy for Marian. Her cousin had fallen hard for the Earl of Harrington. They were happy, and that was all that mattered, but the past year without her cousin at her side every day had grown tedious. Kaitlin desperately needed something to fill her days. Unfortunately, she didn't do well socializing and didn't have many friends. She had two, her cousin, Marian, and Lady Samantha Cain.

Samantha should be arriving soon to accompany her to Marian's for tea. They met at least once a week, but that would soon come to an end. Marian's husband wanted to retire to his estate for the summer months. He needed to be there to see to his tenants and the repairs needed on some of the outbuildings. Kaitlin would miss her cousin terribly. She was already lonely, and soon she'd lose one of the few people left she felt comfortable around.

"What has you so melancholy, my dear," her uncle, the Earl of Coventry asked as he entered the sitting room.

She lifted her lips in a false smile. Kaitlin tried her best to make everything seem all right, even when she felt like she was dying inside. "Lost in thought." She stood and hugged her uncle, then stepped back. He was home more often after a long bout of illness. He still had horrible days, but for the most part, he seemed on the mend. That could be wishful thinking on her part though. "How are you feeling today?"

"Don't worry about me," he said. "I've never felt better."

He was lying, of course. His gait was slightly off, and he relied on his cane more than he used to. Sometimes, she thought his sight was affected, but her uncle had gotten rather talented in disguising most of his symptoms. The Earl of Coventry was a proud man and hated to show any signs of weakness. Kaitlin allowed him the falsehood of pretending he was all right. It was the least she could do for him. "That's wonderful," she said. "Then you won't mind if I leave you alone for the afternoon."

"Off to have tea with Marian?" he asked. "Do give her my regards, and if her rascal of a husband is around, tell him to pay me a visit before they disappear for the summer."

"I'll be happy to deliver that message for you," Samantha said as she breezed into the room. Her dark hair was styled in an elaborate chignon, and her blue eyes sparkled with mischief. She wore a blue muslin walking gown and straw hat with matching blue ribbons. Kaitlin envied her friend. She was vivacious and feared nothing. Sometimes, Kaitlin wished she could be more like her, but that seemed impossible.

Samantha could do anything, say whatever she

wanted, and not once did she care what anyone in society thought of her. No one dared treat her as inconsequential. Kaitlin shied away from everyone and had trouble stringing two words together in polite company. That was why she often stayed on the outskirts of balls and rarely was asked to dance. The only people who paid her any mind were her family and Samantha. She might as well be a marble statue for how little people noticed her. Truthfully, she rather liked being invisible. It saved her from making a fool of herself in society. That was why Samantha often felt it was her responsibility to assist her with even the smallest of tasks. It was her friend's way of easing Kaitlin's comfort. "I'm not sure I need your assistance with such a menial task," she told Samantha. "I'm more than capable of delivering that message to Lord Harrington."

She lifted a brow. "You are still that formal with him?" Her lips twitched. "He is your cousin through marriage. Surely he's given you leave to use his given name."

Her cheeks heated. She hated how she embarrassed so easily. "Of course he has, but it's not proper."

Samantha shook her head. "It's proper because

4

you've been given permission and he's family. Stop overthinking the small things."

"She is right," the earl said. "Jonas wouldn't have allowed you to enter into any sort of impropriety. He's too smitten with Marian to make such a blunder." His lips twitched. "The boy has had some wicked days in the past, but he's almost...*tame* now."

Kaitlin sighed. "I'm not comfortable with it."

"All right," Samantha said. "I'll leave it be, but at least consider loosening those strictures you place on yourself. Learn to live a little."

That was easy for her to do, but never for Kaitlin. Ever since she lost her parents and had to come and live with her uncle, she'd lost all ability to be spontaneous. She'd grown up faster than she'd thought possible. Being an orphan had altered her completely, and not for the better. Instead of telling her friend something she was already aware of, she turned to her uncle. "Take care of yourself while I am away. I'll see you for the evening meal."

"Have fun, dear," he said with fondness in his voice.

She picked up her bonnet and secured it over her light golden hair. It was a white with pale pink ribbons that perfectly matched her gown. Kaitlin turned to Samantha and smiled. "Are you ready to walk over?"

"Of course," she said and grinned. "I've been waiting for this visit all week. I think Marian has news for us."

"Oh?" She tilted her head to the side. "How would you possibly know that without speaking to her."

Samantha looped her arm through hers and leaned down to whisper, "I had my maid bribe Marian's. I do like to keep abreast of things…"

Kaitlin shook her head. "You're incorrigible."

"I know," she replied with an amused tone. "But you love me any way."

They exited the house and headed to Marian's townhouse. Kaitlin, unlike Samantha, could be patient and wait for Marian to tell her whatever news she might have. She had her suppositions too though, and she hoped today was the day Marian trusted them with her secrets.

GREGORY CAIN, THE EARL OF SHELBY WOULD MUCH rather find comfort in the arms of a soft, willing woman than spend even a second in the company of the sniveling idiot currently in front of him.

Regrettably, he wasn't going to be so lucky. The Earl of Barton had to be the biggest, most irritating moron he'd ever had the displeasure of being acquainted with. "How long have you known me?" Gregory's tone was a combination of exasperation and firmness. He hated dealing with the newcomers to Coventry Club. He still didn't know why he agreed to act as Harrington's second in command, so to speak. Gregory shirked responsibility whenever he could, and this was far more than he'd ever allowed himself to take charge of.

"Uh…" Barton's face went blank, and he tilted his head back. "About a month now, I think."

Why the hell had Harrington allowed this child into the club? Surely he had to realize Barton wasn't prepared for the duty and loyalty that came with being a member of the Coventry Club. "You've been welcomed in this club for a month. We've been acquainted much longer than that." He hated to admit that, but Barton's estate was near Gregory's mother's family home in Sussex. "You've been to Parkdale Abbey a few times while we were in residence." Not that he'd visited his mother's family lately. He preferred London and the entertainments it offered. He didn't even bother visiting his own estate much.

The Earl of Barton, the sandy-haired, senseless twit, was almost a decade Gregory's junior. He was maybe four years older than Gregory's sister, Samantha. His green eyes had a dullness to them that didn't give the impression of much intelligence. Perhaps that was his interpretation on the earl's intellect... He certainly hadn't displayed any signs that he held any amount of astuteness.

"I guess..."

Gregory rolled his eyes. He was so done with him. His patience had run thin, and he was about to knock some sense into the idiot when Harrington walked in. He had dark hair that curled around his neck and forehead, and his blue eyes held a keenness that Barton's had lacked. He would have to hold some intelligence to be able to wrangle the lords that graced the club's hallowed walls. The head of the Coventry Club stopped and first glanced at Barton, then at Gregory before he raised a brow arrogantly. "Do I want to know?"

"Probably not," Gregory answered. His fingers twitched, and he fought the urge to clench them together. Harrington should handle this mess, not him. "But you should."

Harrington strolled closer and pulled out a chair to join them. He sat and then placed his elbows on the polished oak table. "What has Barton done now?" He didn't even bother to glance at the young earl's direction.

Gregory groaned. "If you knew he'd be a problem, then pray tell why is…"

"Because it wasn't that long ago the two of us required a guiding hand, and this club provided it." He turned to Barton. "Have you been able to discern why Shelby is irate with you?"

"I…" Barton swallowed hard. "Well, I didn't mean to."

Gregory clenched his fist, but he held back. Barely. His anger was a barely tethered rage. Harrington chuckled lightly but remained composed. He wasn't sure how his friend managed to keep that calm façade, but he envied it. Losing his temper came naturally to Gregory. It was a bit of a family trait he wished had passed him by, but unfortunately, it had become ingrained inside of him at an early age. Gregory glared at him and said in a seething tone, "That doesn't make what you did right."

Harrington pinned Gregory with an unwavering glance. His friend's way of warning him to back off and let him handle his protégée. If one could call Barton that… Then Harrington returned his attention to the ignorant fool and gave Gregory a moment to breathe through his anger. "There are rules we have here. You were told of these rules before you were allowed to become a member. They aren't difficult or extensive, and you are having trouble with the little we have." He motioned to Gregory and said, "Shelby wouldn't be discussing anything with you if you hadn't blundered. So, please tell me, what is it that you're having difficulty understanding?"

Barton sank back into his chair and then stared at Gregory with a mulish expression on his face. Soon he'd be acting like a petulant child. He lifted his chin in a defiant manner and said, "Why can't I have my friends here? They would love to be a part of a swell place like this."

"No one is supposed to know of the club," Gregory reminded him. Why was it so difficult for him to understand? "Your friends, if that's what you must call them, are not members. Those lads you brought here, well, one was a chit, but I digress." The female street urchin had held a bit of beauty to her. If she was cleaned up and let her hair grow out, she'd be stunning. Gregory considered himself a connoisseur of gorgeous women. "What matters is they were pickpockets, thieves, maybe worse.

They were here to rob us blind." Or at least attempt to…

"They were not." He lifted his chin. "They wanted a spot of fun. What is wrong with that?"

"Listen…"

Harrington held up his hand to interrupt Gregory. "This is going to be your only warning, Lord Barton. If this happens again, we won't be so polite. You will be excommunicated from this club. Your key will be handed over, and if you make a fuss, we *will* ruin you. Do you understand?"

He nodded his head frantically. "I'm sorry." He didn't actually look as if he had any remorse for his actions. Barton seemed to be mimicking the words he thought he was supposed to say. If Gregory had to pinpoint exactly what he believed Barton actually felt, it was more fear than anything. Harrington could be scary at times.

"I'm sure you are," Harrington said a mix of sternness and cajoling in his tone. Gregory wasn't sure how Harrington managed sounding both at the same time. "Don't make me regret allowing you into the club. Now go before I decide you're a bad bet after all."

The Earl of Barton hopped to his feet and ran from the room. Gregory clenched his teeth together, glaring in his direction. Then he turned to Harrington and said, "He should have been told to hand in his key immediately."

"Sometimes it is wise to give a person a second chance," Harrington said softly. "Why must you always take the most difficult path?"

He shrugged. "I'm contrary that way."

His friend grinned. "I realized that years ago." Harrington stood. "What are your plans for the afternoon?"

"I'm going to go crawl in my bed upstairs and sleep until nightfall. I fully intend to drink all night and find a few willing ladies to join me in my bed for a bit of…" Gregory lifted his lips upward into a wicked smile as he thought about what he intended to do with his favorite courtesans. "…wanton pleasure."

Harrington stared at him a moment and then silently shook his head. He glanced back at him and said, "Walk with me back to the townhouse. I'd like to speak with you about a few things regarding the club, and Marian is expecting me back soon."

Gregory frowned. "I'd rather not, but all right."

"Rather not what?" Asthey asked nonchalantly as he strolled into the room. His blond hair was a little wind blown and his blue eyes held a hint of mischievousness in them.

"Take a leisurely stroll," Gregory said in disgust. "Care to join us? Harrington makes it seem positively riveting."

"I did no such thing," Harrington said, sounding offended. "You give the impression that I've become tame or something."

Asthey lifted a mocking brow. "You have become an old married fellow now."

Gregory chuckled, at ease for the first time that day. "Well, he does make a valid observation."

"Bugger off," Harrington said and glared at both of them. "Are you coming with me or not? I might as well talk to you both and gain your opinion." Then he met Gregory's gaze. "Or are you going to continue to be difficult?"

He really was tired. It had been a long night and an even longer day. Gregory hated dealing with some of the more idiotic members of the club. Sleep would be heaven, and later, after he rested, he fully intended to spend some quality time with some of his favorite courtesans. Harrington was a good friend. He could indulge him and get some exercise before he napped. "Fine, I'll accompany you,"

Gregory conceded. "I'll try to be...less problematic, but I'm not making any promises."

They exited the club together as they often did, but some things were still different. Gregory and Asthey were unmarried and welcome in the club. Harrington was allowed because he ran it, despite his marriage. Asthey was making noise about wanting to find a wife, but Gregory wasn't ready for such a commitment. He wasn't sure what he would do once Asthey found a wife. It would alter a lot in his life, and he hated change. Gregory had a feeling that, very soon, everything he had grown accustomed to would be ripped apart. Time would tell how well he dealt with it...

CHAPTER 2

a maid brought in a tea tray and set it on a nearby table. It was already filled with little cakes and pastries. Samantha stood and walked over to the table as the maid exited. "Would you like me to serve?" she asked.

Marian nodded. "If you insist." She turned to Kaitlin. "Are you ready for tea?"

Kaitlin glanced over at Samantha and then back at Marian. They had been at Marian's townhouse for an hour now and her cousin still had said nothing of import. It had been all gossip and talk about the weather. She was growing bored with their discourse. Surely Marian would tell them her good news soon. "Tea would be lovely," she said. Kaitlin didn't make a scene. She'd always been the quiet one, and she was all right with that.

Samantha poured tea into two cups and prepared each one how they liked it. Kaitlin liked hers a little sweet and Marian preferred a splash of milk. After the tea was ready, she carried over the cups on saucers and handed them to them. Kaitlin held the saucer in her hand and lifted the teacup in the other. She sipped on the tea and then closed her eyes in pleasure. There was nothing like a decent cup of tea. "It's perfect."

Samantha picked up her own cup and then sat next to Kaitlin on the settee. "Now that we're all in possession of refreshments perhaps Marian can quit stalling and tell us her big announcement."

Marian had been mid sip when Samantha made that statement. She started to cough and waved her hand in front of her face. Kaitlin took her cup and set it on a nearby table then went back to her. "Are you all right?"

"I'm fine." She wheezed out the words as she coughed some more. "Need to catch...my...breath."

Kaitlin frowned and glared up at Samantha. "You have no patience."

"I never claimed to have any." She shrugged lightly.

Marian managed to get her breathing under control. She held her hand up to her throat and tapped at it a little. "How do you know?" She narrowed her gaze and pinned Samantha with it. "And next time, please show some consideration and wait long enough for me to actually swallow the sip of tea before you make such a frank statement."

Kaitlin's lips twitched. Some things never really changed... "Since you are clearly able to breathe properly now, I don't suppose you can explain to me what Samantha is referring to?"

"I'm..." She took a deep breath and then continued, "expecting..."

"Expecting what?" Kaitlin asked, and then Samantha started laughing. "*Oh*... Please forget I asked that." She felt a little bit ignorant for even broaching the topic. Especially when she suspected that Marian was enceinte. She didn't understand why she hadn't made an announcement yet.

Marian smiled. "We've been trying for a while now." Her cheeks turned pink as she spoke. "But, uh..."

"Say no more." Samantha grinned. "We can infer from that."

"Jonas is thrilled, as am I," she said. "And a little scared."

Kaitlin sat back down on the settee. Now that she knew Marian would be fine, she didn't see any reason to stand around. Besides, she had no idea what to add to this conversation. She didn't expect she'd ever marry. No one noticed her. For a brief time, she thought perhaps the Earl of Asthey might court her, but he abruptly stopped paying her any attention. Though she supposed she could be interpreting his actions incorrectly.

She didn't know anything about gentlemen or how to flirt with them. That was more Samantha's forte. *She* didn't have any trouble gaining a gentleman's attention. Samantha's problem was her brother, the Earl of Shelby. He scared off most of her suitors and made finding a husband difficult for her friend.

"Don't worry about a thing," Samantha said with a wave of her hand. "I'll help where I can."

"Sam," Marian said with a shocked tone to her voice. "You're an innocent. I can't have you anywhere near this pregnancy. It…"

"Don't be a nitwit," Samantha said. "I've read plenty of books on the subject and so has Kaitlin."

Marian turned to glance at Kaitlin. *Drat.* Why did Samantha have to sell her out? She'd gotten curious and studied some of Marian's medical journals. They were fascinating, and she was finally starting to understand why Marian wished to be a doctor. Not that Kaitlin desired the same thing. Some of the things she'd learned about the human body was… disgusting. She'd rather not deal with any of that. "I am not certain I understand what Samantha is implying." Maybe she could pretend ignorance. No one, except the two ladies with her in the room, would ever question her. Because they didn't actually notice her…

"Don't play the sly chit with us," Samantha chastised her. "You may be shy and quiet as a mouse in public, but we have seen your more hoydenish side."

She crinkled her nose. "I'm never a hoyden. Don't be ridiculous. That word describes you more than it has ever defined me."

"I've always thought of her as a hellion myself," a male with a deep rich baritone said as he entered the room.

They all turned toward the sound. Three gentlemen stood in the entrance. One was Lord Harrington, Marian's husband. The other two were his closest friends, Lord Shelby and Lord Asthey. The one that had spoken was Samantha's brother, Shelby.

"You have no room to censure me in any fashion considering your own roguish behavior." Samantha glared at her brother.

"Well," Shelby began. He stopped briefly and winked at Kaitlin. He'd caught her staring at him... Why did he have to be so gorgeous? His hair was as dark as sin itself, and his eyes were so blue they almost sparkled. Probably from all the mischief he partook in. "Why should I stop doing something I am quite proficient with? It would devastate the ladies..."

"Do *not* finish that sentence," Samantha commanded as she stepped toward Shelby.

The Earl of Harrington ran his hand through his chestnut locks and sighed. "Sheathe your claws," he said. "I'd rather not have any bloodshed or disturbance of any kind in front of my wife."

Samantha calmed down at his words. "All right. I'll concede this isn't where I should have this conversation with my brother." Shelby's lips twitched into a sinful smile. Kaitlin's heart stirred a little. He was so handsome and charming... Samantha didn't notice her brother's smile though. It would be awkward if she had. She wagged her finger at him though as if lecturing a small child. "After all,

I wouldn't want to be responsible for anything happening to Marian or the baby."

"Marian's having a baby?" Asthey said with a shocked tone. "Why am I always the last to know."

Kaitlin sighed. High tea had taken an unexpected turn. Clearly Jonas and Marian hadn't been quite ready to impart their good tidings yet. Samantha needed to learn when to hold her tongue and when to speak. Something Kaitlin doubted she'd ever quite master...

GREGORY INWARDLY GROANED. IF HARRINGTON WAS going to be a father, that changed everything... His marriage had been the first step in that direction, and now, Harrington had ensured he'd be forever tied to home and hearth. He didn't blame his friend. Harrington loved his wife, and in some ways, Gregory was jealous of that. Oh, he didn't want a wife or children, but he liked the idea of love.

He'd realized early on something as enormous as love would not be part of his life. That would be more responsibility than Gregory ever wanted to tangle with. He had several vices, but his favorites were an unending supply of brandy and wanton women. He'd likely have to give up the first if he married and undoubtedly would have to give up the second. A wife liked a husband who doted on her. He shuddered at the possibility. Sure, there were plenty of ton marriages that didn't have love in them, but if he ever shackled himself to a woman, he wanted something more than a business arrangement. He had no desire to experience a cold bed with a bit of unhappiness thrown in.

Gregory glanced at Asthey and upbraided him, "Don't be surly." Then he set his gaze upon his sister and glared at her. "I could be wrong, but that is probably a secret no one should have been privy to yet."

Samantha rolled her eyes. "How was I to know Lord Harrington didn't trust his own friends with his good news."

Sometimes he wanted to strangle his sister. If he didn't love her, he might have when they were children. "Perhaps," he began. "It would have behooved you to keep a secret that isn't yours to tell." Acerbity etched through every word he spoke.

Gregory stepped toward his sister, but Lady Kaitlin Evans stepped in front of him. "Lord Shelby," she said in a shaky tone. "Would you like some tea?"

"Tea?" He stared at her uncertain what game she

played. "No, I don't want tea." Lady Kaitlin usually didn't speak to him. He didn't want to be rude to her either. She was a shy mouse who unfortunately allowed his sister to browbeat her into activities she wouldn't otherwise participate in. "Please step aside."

"No," she replied defiantly. "I must insist you not have a row with your sister. The excitement might prove too difficult for Marian, and we must consider her condition."

Gregory inwardly cringed and worked to calm himself down. "I'd never hurt my own sister."

Lady Kaitlin nodded. "I do realize that, my lord, but a raised voice is not unheard of between the two of you."

"She is right," Asthey said. "I've witnessed more disagreements between you and Lady Samantha than any person should be subjected to."

"Ahem," Lady Marian cleared her throat. "Perhaps Kaitlin has the right of it. If tea isn't to your liking, perhaps Jonas can pour you a spot of brandy instead."

Lord Harrington met his wife's gaze and then returned his attention to Gregory and Asthey. "Perhaps we can continue our conversation in my study."

"No," Gregory said, dismissing Harrington's

suggestion. "I'd like to stay here with the ladies." He turned toward Lady Marian. "If you'll accept my apologies and felicitations on your good news."

"Of course," Lady Marian said amiably. She looked at Harrington. "Brandy for the men and tea for the ladies."

Harrington nodded and went to a nearby decanter, where he filled three glasses then handed one to Asthey. He went back and picked up the other two glasses and carried one over to Gregory. "I promise I'll behave," he told his friend. Gregory lifted his glass and held it high. "A toast to the future Harrington heir."

"You don't know it'll be a boy," Harrington said.

"Either way, it's happy tidings, and we should celebrate."

They all held their drinks high and toasted to the birth of Lord and Lady Harrington's first child. Gregory sipped his brandy. It burned nicely as it slid down his throat. Harrington and Asthey had wandered off to the side of the room and were deep in a conversation. He didn't really care to discern what they were talking about. He leaned against the wall and continued to sip his brandy. It was the safest course of action considering how he's almost lost control of his temper again.

He had to work harder on keeping it reined. Gregory hated how easy it was for him to give into his barely tethered rage. He glanced around the room. Samantha and Lady Marian had their heads together discussing something, and he prayed his sister was receiving a lecture she might actually listen to.

Lady Kaitlin sat by herself in a chair near the other two ladies. She didn't speak and hadn't even sipped her tea. Gregory was intrigued, but didn't act on it. He could easily go speak to her. Chastise her for stepping in front of him on the brink of a rage, but he didn't have the right to do such a thing. Lady Kaitlin was not his relation, and he certainly didn't want to court her. He was the last person that should ever court a lady, and definitely not one so benevolent as Lady Kaitlin Evans. She deserved far better than the likes of him. So he stayed where he was and resigned himself to a long lonely life.

CHAPTER 3

There were a handful of social events remaining for the season. Of course, there would be some summer house parties to attend, but for the most part, Kaitlin would be free from obligations. Still, she wasn't so sure that would be good for her. When left alone, she tended to withdraw into herself, and without Marian or Samantha to urge her to explore the outside world, Kaitlin doubted she'd leave the townhouse. Her heart raced and her stomach fluttered at the very idea of socializing. If she had any chance of finding a husband, she had to find a way of overcoming her anxiety.

"What has ye lost in thought?" her maid asked in a heavy Scottish accent. Mollie was twisting Kaitlin's hair into an elaborate chignon. Soon she would have to leave for the Loxton end of the season ball.

"It's nothing," she said nonchalantly as she stared at herself blandly in the looking glass. Kaitlin often spoke with her maid in a less formal way. She relied on Mollie to help dress her and present herself in the best way possible. In some ways, Mollie was her closest friend. Yes, Kaitlin was close to Samantha and Marian. She could tell them anything, but sometimes she felt—alone. They were not with her nearly as much as Mollie. Kaitlin relied on her maid for so much. "Maybe we should do something more with my hair."

"Such as?"

She swallowed hard. Kaitlin didn't know why it was so difficult for her to voice anything she truly wanted. If she was uncertain, it was even worse. "My mother's pearl comb or her sapphire diadem."

"The diadem would match yer eyes and compliment yer gown," Mollie said thoughtfully. "I'll retrieve it and pin it securely into yer hair." She finished fastening Kaitlin's blonde locks into place, then went to retrieve the jeweled headband. She brought it back and placed it over her hair so it resembled a cerulean crown sparkling against her golden hair. "There," Mollie said. "Yer simply beautiful, my lady. Stand up now and we'll get ye into yer dress."

Kaitlin did as she directed as Mollie retrieved her indigo gown. It was one of Kaitlin's favorite dresses. It was a deep blue silk overlapping ivory silk in the center and trimmed with silver ribbons and tiny seed pearls along the bodice. She stepped into the gown and then Mollie pulled it up over her chemise. Kaitlin slipped her arms into the short, ruffled sleeves. Mollie fastened all the tiny buttons and tied the silk ribbon at top edge of the bodice into a billowy bow against her back. "There you're all ready. All you need is to slide on your dancing slippers, and you can meet Lady Marian in the foyer."

Her cousin acted as her chaperone now that she was considered a matron. They no longer needed anyone to accompany them, but Lord Harrington often attended the functions Marian chose to attend. Neither one of them liked being separated from each other, and Kaitlin found that habit of theirs sweet. Maybe one day she'd find someone to love her too.

She went to the chair on the far side of the room where her slippers were. Kaitlin lifted the edge of her gown and slid her left foot into the first slipper and repeated the action with her other foot. "Thank you, Mollie," she said. "Enjoy your evening. I'll see you when I return home."

"Have a wonderful time, my lady," she told her. "Do try to dance. A pretty lass shouldn't spend the entire evening in the corner."

"No promises," Kaitlin replied solemnly. She rarely danced, and she spent more times sitting in the corner watching than she liked to admit. Mollie listened to her bemoan her fate and hated that Kaitlin didn't try to be more social. It wasn't in her nature to be the diamond that stood out amongst all the other ladies in attendance. No one noticed her, and most of the time she was all right with that. Sometimes though she wished one of the gentlemen would glance her way and take a risk. Even when she wasn't brave enough to do it herself.

"One day you'll meet a man who sees you for the beautiful, kind, lady you are, and he'll find himself unable to look away again."

"Perhaps." Kaitlin doubted it. "That day may never come though, and I will have to accept that I am meant to be alone." That hurt to admit and actually say aloud. "My brother will marry some day, and I'll be a wonderful spinster aunt."

"Nonsense." Mollie pursed her lips up in displeasure and shook her head defiantly. "Yer meant for more than that. Not that ye won't be a lovely auntie to Lord Frossly's children, but ye need bairns of yer own."

Kaitlin sighed. She would love to have a family of her own. That would prove difficult if she couldn't manage to come out of the shadows and find a gentleman to marry. Flirting was too hard, and she failed at it every time she attempted. "Trust me, it's better this way. This mythical gentleman doesn't exist." She headed to the door. "Now I really must leave. Marian will be here soon, and I don't want to keep her waiting."

"Fine," Mollie said, her voice indicating she was upset with her. "But I do believe ye will find love. Once ye open yerself up to it, it will find you. The trouble is ye are unable to imagine yourself in love or a gentleman loving ye."

Marian didn't bother replying to that. She feared that her maid was very much correct. If she allowed herself to dream of love—and a handsome gentleman willing to give her his heart as he deftly stole her—it would probably lead to empty promises and a broken heart. Kaitlin wasn't the type gentleman loved or fought for. She didn't inspire anything from anyone. She was the very definition of wallflower. Unnoticeable, unremarkable, and unworthy of their attention.

GREGORY SAT IN THE CARD ROOM AT THE LOXTON ball staring at the cards that had been dealt him. He was going to win, but it didn't make him happy. Nothing sparked anything remotely joyful in him anymore. He should leave the ball and go back to the club. At least there he could find something less sedate to entertain himself with. He wasn't even certain why he'd decided to attend the ball. Samantha didn't need him to chaperone her. She could have accompanied Harrington and his wife. His friend wouldn't have minded looking after Gregory's sister.

Not that Gregory made that great of a chaperone. For the most part, he allowed Samantha to do as she pleased. He'd already made it known to the gentlemen of the ton that, if they overstepped, they'd pay a steep price. He'd had to participate in one duel and two bouts of fisticuffs to make sure the message was understood. It helped that one of the gentlemen who Gregory had pummeled had been one of his friends, the Earl of

Darcy. The earl hadn't understood why Gregory had objected to him courting Samantha. Darcy wasn't really interested in a love match with Samantha, and Gregory had seen that quite clearly. Now that Darcy was happily married, perhaps he did comprehend why Gregory had been so adamant against his courtship.

"Are you playing or not, Shelby?" Prince Luca Dragomir glared at him over his cards. "Or are you going to stare at your cards the rest of the evening."

Gregory lifted a brow allowing his indifference to be quite clear, then with elaborate care, he picked a card and set it firmly on the table. "I believe that's the match gentleman." They all cursed and threw the rest of their cards on the table.

"You have all the bloody luck," the Duke of Ashley mumbled. A strand of his golden blond hair fell over his forehead, and he quickly pushed it back. "I can't wait until something brings you down low."

"It'll be more accurate to state we cannot wait until he meets a lady that will turn his world upside down." The prince replied and then sneered. "Perhaps we should place a wager on it."

Gregory lifted is lips into a cocky half smile. "Do as you feel you must, but I'd save your funds. I'm never marrying or falling in love. I'll leave that fate to you saps." He stood and nodded at them all.

"Now, if you'll pardon me, I must check on my sister."

He didn't intend to do anything of the sort, but it sounded like a likely excuse for departing. They wouldn't believe him if he said he was developing a sad case of ennui.

Prince Luca brushed a hand through his dark hair, smoothing it back. "It'll be even more satisfying when you fall." He turned to the duke. "A hundred quid he'll meet her before the season ends." Shelby held back from rolling his eyes. The prince would have to return home sometime. He returned to England so his wife could visit her family.

The duke chuckled. "You don't have a lot of faith in that wager if you're only betting one hundred quid. I'll raise you and say one hundred pounds that he's already met her. Though I doubt he has realized it yet."

The prince held out his hand to the duke. "I accept." Then he turned and met Gregory's gaze. "Do you wish to bet on yourself?"

Gregory's smile was all teeth when he lifted his lips. "As a rule, I don't make bad bets. Not everyone desires wedded bliss. Go home to your wives and be happy they deign to suffer your company." He spun on his heels to leave the two gentlemen alone. He didn't have time for their nonsense. Let them make their wagers. What did he care?

He turned the corner and nearly knocked a lady to the ground. He reached out and placed his arms around her waist and pulled her upright before she tumbled downward. He hadn't seen her face, but what he'd been able to feel...was...bloody hell. He shouldn't be noticing anything about a lady at the Loxton ball. That would lead him nowhere. Unless she was an unhappily married matron or widow... Then he could charm his way into her bed.

Gregory glanced up with a hopeful gaze and his heart sank low. This was one lady he had to keep his hands off of. If he did anything remotely untoward, he'd find himself in front of a parson faster than he could blink. Harrington would have his head. "Lady Kaitlin. Please accept my apologies. I should have been watching where I stepped."

He blinked several times. When had she turned into a fetching beauty? He'd done his best to never fully pay any attention to her. Now he wished he hadn't taken the time to really look at her. She had gorgeous golden hair and brilliant blue eyes. Her face was...perfect. Delicate and heart-shaped with delectable, quite kissable, pink lips. He mentally shook that thought away. He would not be putting his lips anywhere near hers.

"It's all right, Lord Shelby," she said demurely. "No one notices me."

"What?" He let go of her once he was certain she was steady on her feet. "Don't be ridiculous. Trust me, they notice you. Otherwise, they're all blind." Like he'd been...

She smiled and it lit up her entire face. She was so bloody beautiful... He had to put some distance between them and fast. He would not be seducing an innocent miss. It wasn't done. "You do not need to be kind. I'm a wallflower, and I've accepted that."

He frowned. Gregory didn't like her talking in such a disparaging tone about herself. "Why do you believe this?"

"I'm on my fourth season. It's enough evidence at my failure to be remarkable." She shrugged lightly. "I doubt I could change anything now."

"Perhaps you haven't met the right gentleman?"

"Or perhaps I already have, but he's too preoccupied to notice I exist," she answered. "Don't fret about something that is unchangeable."

Gregory hated that she believed any of this about herself. He wished there was a way to bolster how she perceived herself. There were only so many things Gregory could do, and he wasn't about to ask for her hand. "That doesn't mean I must like any of it. I wish I could make a difference in some fashion."

She tilted her head to the side. "Why would you want to? I'm no one to you."

"Don't be ridiculous," he chastised her. "You're my sister's closest friend...or at least one of them. I'd like to think that we are at the very least acquaintances, maybe more than that if you'd allow it." He hadn't meant to say that last bit aloud. He mentally cursed himself for letting those words spill out of his mouth.

"There you go being kind again, my lord," Lady Kaitlin said softly. "I do like the idea of you as a friend. As my *friend,* do you think you could help me with one small thing?"

"Of course," he answered readily, wanting to assist her in any way he could. He'd never felt so useless. Her serenity soothed him where he'd been restless before crossing paths with her.

She bit down on her lips plumping them even more. He nearly groaned at the sight. She glanced away. "Never mind. Forget I asked anything."

"No," he said. "I insist. Tell me what you need."

Why did she feel as if she couldn't ask him for aid

ONE LESS SCANDALOUS EARL

now? He wanted her to trust him. Gregory didn't even understand why now.

"I shouldn't," she began her voice a little wobbly as she spoke. "It's that... I never..."

"What?" he asked.

"Kiss me," she said softly, and he nearly jerked away at her words. It was almost as if she'd read his mind. Surely she understood why they couldn't... Especially not here, in the hall between the ballroom and the card room—anyone could walk in on them, and then... He'd be trapped.

CHAPTER 4

Kaitlin swallowed the lump that had formed in her throat. She glanced up into the Earl of Shelby's normally cold blue eyes. His gaze usually froze her in place, but something was different today. They burned. It set ablaze within her a need she hadn't known existed. She blamed that desire on the words she'd blurted out.

Kiss me...

What had she been thinking? Clearly, she'd lost all ability to employ proper etiquette. A lady did not ask a gentleman to kiss her. Especially not a notable rake... That request begged him to ruin her, and heaven help her—she'd gladly risk everything for one kiss from him.

"Please forget I asked." She fought tears as she

attempted to move past him and failed. Kaitlin stumbled, and he caught her before she hit the ground.

"You really need to stop falling at my feet. It might give me the wrong impression." His tone was light and mischievous.

Was he mocking her? How mortifying... Kaitlin couldn't look at him again because she might lose control of her emotions if she did. She was such a fool. She kept her face averted away from his as she spoke. "Thank you, my lord." She pushed away from him, but he held her close.

"Why do you wish for me to kiss you?"

Because he was handsome, charming, and she'd loved him from afar for more years than she could recall. "Because I'd like to understand to... experience what it feels like at least once."

"You don't think your eventual husband can share that with you?" He lifted her chin and forced her to meet his gaze. "Shouldn't he have that right? To teach you what a kiss can do."

She shook her head defiantly. "That mythical man has yet to appear, and I'm tired of waiting. I've decided this will be my last season. If you won't do it, I'll find someone else more willing."

She wouldn't, but it sounded good. Perhaps it

would inspire him to give her what she wished for. His mouth on hers—it might not be as passionate as it could be. He didn't truly desire her. No man had shown any signs they did, and a rogue of Shelby's caliber had more options than most.

"You'll do no such thing." His nostrils flared a bit as he clearly seethed with barely contained temper. Kaitlin tried to take a step back, but he wouldn't allow it. He kept her at his side with his arm looped around her. If only she hadn't almost fallen… "You need a husband, and lucky for you, I'm willing to help you find one."

"I don't require your assistance." She would not let this man find her a husband. That would be a blow her heart couldn't withstand.

"I must disagree." He pulled her flush against his hard body. Her heart raced in her chest. She'd never been this close to a man. Kaitlin wanted to be even closer. Heat filled her cheeks, and her female parts nearly throbbed with a need she didn't understand. Shelby lowered his head until their noses nearly touched. All he had to do was move a little more, and he'd be able to press his lips to hers. Kaitlin's breath hitched as she waited for him to close the distance, but he didn't kiss her. "You definitely need a keeper. Ladies don't ask notorious rakes to kiss them. Not innocent ones anyway, or are you more experienced then I've been led to believe?"

"I…" she stumbled over the words. "I've never been kissed. Is it so bad to want one? Or am I never to feel anything? I will be a spinster soon, and I wished for one small thing." She licked her lips, and he groaned. Perhaps he wasn't so unaffected as he pretended to be. "It's unfortunate that I've disgusted you with the idea of a kiss, but you need not concern yourself. I'm certain another gentleman will find me appealing. I'm not that unpleasant."

"I already told you that is out of the question. You will not go around London asking every eligible gentleman or rogue to kiss you. That would be scandalous."

She lifted a brow. "Well, I suppose you would understand a scandal far better than anyone."

"Everything I've done is above reproach. No one…"

"Would dare gossip about you?" Her lips tilted upward into an uninhibited smile. "Now who is being obtuse? The entire ton discusses your prowess in the, uh, bedchamber. I'm innocent, not deaf."

Horror spread over his face. What did he think all the ladies discussed behind closed doors? The weather? "Ladies…"

"Are the worst gossips," she interrupted him. "They don't have any compunction about keeping their dalliances quiet. Especially the ones that have visited your bed." She'd had mixed feelings listening or rather eavesdropping on those conversations. Kaitlin had never known jealousy until she'd heard in detail how the Earl of Shelby was a wonderful lover. She had wanted to scratch the bragging ladies' eyes out.

Not long after that, it had become a game amongst Shelby's conquests. They would share tales about their night with him, determined to be the lady he would choose to come back to for another night of passion. Shelby didn't visit a lady's bed twice. That had been the one thing that eased her jealousy. He didn't love any of them. They had been nothing more than a convenience. "Now, if you'll let me go, I'll leave you alone. I would hate to take too much of your time."

"We're not done," he insisted. "We still need to discuss your penchant for propositioning scoundrels."

Kaitlin sighed. "I promise all the gentleman at the ball are free from my unwanted attentions. At least for tonight... You don't need to keep me company."

"That's not encouraging." He leaned down so his

mouth brushed against her ear. "But as I said, you're in luck. I am going to help you whether you like it or not."

"Why are you being so difficult? I've given you plenty of reasons to let this be." She closed her eyes and reveled in his closeness. She might never have his arms around her again. It was a conundrum. She wanted to run and pull him closer at the same time.

He stepped back and she immediately felt the loss. She'd been warm, and now her body felt as if it had lost something essential to its survival. She wanted him to move back to her. Hold her. Love her.

"Because you're a dear friend to my sister. She would want you to find happiness." He frowned. "I'm not being difficult. You're the one not seeing what a gift my assistance would be for you."

He wasn't wrong. Samantha did want her to find love. To finally fall in love and discover true happiness… Both Samantha and her cousin Marian hoped she'd find it. Kaitlin was more practical. She wanted a moment of passion. That had been what prompted her to ask Shelby to kiss her. If she was only going to have one kiss, she wanted it to be a good one, and there was no other man she believed could make her feel even an ounce of wild unrelenting desire. It had to be him or no one, but she wasn't going to tell him that. The man already had an overinflated ego. "Pardon me if I don't find your offer to be appealing. Don't strain yourself for me."

"It's not like that. You're making it sound as if it is a chore. Trust me it wouldn't be."

Being near him and not having him? That had been torturous for quite a while now. Even when it had seemed as if Asthey might court her, she never stopped hoping Shelby would notice her. He was always polite. Samantha pushed him and he made biting comments to her, but that was more or less sibling bickering. Kaitlin never doubted that Shelby adored his sister. "It would be more difficult for me if you decided to find me a husband." She folded her arms over her chest. "Correct me if I am incorrect, or did you not dissuade all the eligible gentleman that it would be to their best interest to not court your sister."

"That's different. They don't deserve her."

"Is that so?" She lifted a brow and seethed inside. "But I do?"

His eyes widened briefly, and then he shook his head. For a moment, he had looked...stunned. As if he couldn't believe she'd dare to question his words and actions. "That's not what I meant..." He slid his hand over his dark locks with agitation. "I'm blundering when I don't mean to."

She should take pity on him, but she'd had enough of this conversation. He wanted to find her a husband as a consolation prize. Shelby didn't want to kiss her, so he was doing what he deemed the next best thing. Finding her a man who might want to instead. "That may be so, but it doesn't make my concerns any less valid. Any gentleman who believes I am under your protection will give me a wide berth. Your help will not aid me in finding a husband. Add that to my awkwardness during social occasions, and its not a good mix."

He scrunched his eyebrows together. "I don't understand why they overlook you. You're a beautiful woman and should have your pick of the eligible marriage-minded gentleman." How nice of him. He thought she was pretty enough that she should be able to find a husband. She wouldn't roll her eyes at him, and she'd at least attempt to hold back the sarcasm from her voice. What she really heard with his words was—*you're not pretty enough for me, and I sure as hell am not marrying anyone, especially you.* She wasn't good enough for the Earl of Shelby. Not even for a pity kiss...

"While I appreciate your kind assessment of my

outwardly attributes that oversimplifies the situation. I'm a wallflower. The idea of conversation with someone I'm not familiar with terrifies me. My inability to even make small talk is off-putting. Asking you for anything..." Kaitlin swallowed the lump that formed in her throat. "Especially a kiss." She shook her head. "You don't know how difficult that was for me. I doubt you could ever understand what it is like to struggle every day to attend a ball or hold a simple conversation. So don't you dare pass judgment on me. I don't need your interpretation of my life." She'd given up on any chance at marriage. Besides, she didn't want any other gentleman. If she couldn't have Shelby, no one else would do. Not even Asthey. Sure, he was handsome enough, but he didn't make her heart race.

"You need a little push. I can help you with that."

She blew out a breath. "No. Just no."

"You must see that a kiss between us wouldn't do. It's...wrong."

That was almost like a slap in the face. She'd suspected he didn't desire her, but to have it verbally thrown at her. Kaitlin wanted to cry even more than ever. "Certainly," she replied curtly. "I wouldn't want to make you uncomfortable."

She turned to leave but he reached for her again.

He'd wrapped his hand around her arm and turned her to face him. His gaze was filled with emotions she couldn't quite identify. "It's not you, sprite. I'm no good for an innocent. My soul was darkened long ago, and I'd never dirty you with my touch."

Her heart softened a little at his words. He didn't deem himself worthy of her, not the other way around. There had to be a way to persuade him against that way of thinking. He was everything she wasn't. "I'm not brave enough to embroil myself in society any longer. It's too difficult for me. I could never be the social butterfly that Samantha is."

"You don't need to be," he insisted. "Tell me what gentleman sparks your interest, and I'll ensure he notices you."

"I won't have you browbeat a gentleman into courting me." She didn't want anyone other than Shelby, and she wouldn't dare confess that the man she wanted was him. She didn't want to see a sympathetic look on his face. She couldn't handle him knowing the truth.

"I won't have to." His lips turned upward into a wicked grin. "The gentlemen leave Samantha alone because I'm her brother, and I made my wishes known. I have a right to make those demands."

"I don't think I understand what you're trying to tell me." She tilted her head to the side.

"I don't have any real claims on you. If they see I have an interest in you, they'll want to understand why I am suddenly paying attention to a marriageable lady. They'll see it as a challenge and want to steal away the one lady I might want to keep."

And Shelby didn't stay with any one lady longer than a night... "I see." She really did understand. "What if there is a particular gentleman I'd like to notice me?" An idea was forming in her head. She needed a man to court her that Shelby might see as his equal and spark a hint of jealousy in him. There was a chance it wouldn't work, but she had to try something.

"Then we will work toward you securing that match," he insisted. "Will you allow me to help now?"

"You don't want to know what gentleman I wish to court me?" She would never tell him that it was him she wanted. It would spook him.

"The whom doesn't matter tonight." He winked. "The first step is gaining every gentleman's attention."

"How do we do that?" If this little plot of his kept him at her side, she would do as he asked. At least until she had no choice but to tell him the truth. She loved him, and he was the sole man she'd ever agree to marry.

"The waltz," he said. "And the strands of one is about to start." He held out his hand. "Lady Kaitlin, will you do me the honor of partnering me in the next set?"

He wanted her to dance with him? Her heart leapt in her chest as she placed her hand in his. "It would be my honor."

They walked to the dance floor, and he twirled her around it. This was something she'd dreamed of, and the reality was far better than she could ever have imagined. Shelby had a plan, but so did Kaitlin. Time and perseverance would determine which one prevailed.

CHAPTER 5

The afternoon sun shone bright in the sky and helped warm the chill left over from the morning. Lady Silverly had planned a picnic for that day, and Kaitlin intended to take a carriage to her estate. It was located on the outskirts of London and had a lovely pond she found tranquil. Considering how many members of the ton Lady Silverly invited, that was no easy feat. Kaitlin appreciated any opportunity to escape from the crowd that congregated at any social gathering.

She'd been jubilant since the Loxton ball. Dancing with Lord Shelby had been even better than she could have imagined. He refused to discuss any potential suitors with her. After their dance he deposited her next to Marian and then left the ball.

Considering he never danced with any lady eligible or not, that one dance had the gossip mills buzzing. She hadn't really believed him when he'd suggested that gentleman would flock to her side because he deigned to dance with her. Not long after he departed, her dance card had quickly filled up. Why did dancing with the Earl of Shelby make that much of a difference?

"Where are you off to today?" Her Uncle Charles asked.

She turned and smiled at him. "Lady Silverly's picnic. How are you feeling today, Uncle Charles?"

"It's been a good day." He stared past her as the door opened and Marian entered. "Ah, there's my girl." He walked over and hugged his daughter. "Is Harrington attending this picnic with you?"

Marian stepped back and smiled up at her father. "He'll join us later. He had some business to take care of at the club."

"Good," he said. "I don't like my two girls being alone."

"We're capable of seeing ourselves to and from a picnic," Marian chastised him. "But you needn't worry. We won't be alone." She turned to Kaitlin. "Are you ready to depart?"

Kaitlin picked up her straw bonnet and tied the

dark blue ribbon around her chin. "I am," she answered her cousin. She hugged her uncle and followed Marian out the door.

Marian had a phaeton with a matching pair of grays parked in front of the entrance to the Coventry Townhouse. She hopped inside and waited for Marian to do the same. "Your husband trusts you to drive his precious phaeton?"

"Jonas has come to realize it is in his best interest not to disagree with me when I decide I want to do something. It's much easier to let me have my way." She winked and then flicked the reins to make the horses move. "I can be, um, persuasive."

"I'm not certain I wish to know the methods you utilize to influence your husband to your way of thinking."

Marian nearly glowed with happiness. Soon she'd have a baby and her family would be complete. Kaitlin wanted that. She craved it in ways she hadn't thought possible. Not long ago, she'd been ready to give up and accept her life as a spinster. She had hope now. Somehow, she'd managed a moment of courage, and while it hadn't yielded the results she'd hoped for, it might lead to something better. The Earl of Shelby wished to help her find a husband.

She hoped to convince him he was perfect for the role.

The carriage rolled across the graveled path. It rocked back and forth in a motion that lulled her. Marian remained silent as she focused on keeping the grays on the path. Kaitlin was all right with that. It gave her time to think and plan her next move. Should she tell Shelby she'd decided upon a gentleman as she'd indicated the night before or play coy. Perhaps it would be best to wait and decide.

The trip from Mayfair to the outskirts of London where the Silverly picnic was being held took at least a half hour. Kaitlin had been so lost in her own mind that time passed without her realizing it. Marian pulled the carriage up to the front entrance. A footman greeted them, "My ladies." He bowed. "Would you like me to see to your conveyance?"

"Yes, please," Marian said. She handed him the reins and exited the carriage. Kaitlin followed behind her.

"If you follow the stone path around the house, you'll find where the tents are set up with food. There are servants there to assist you." The footman nodded at them. "Be careful on the path. It can be steep in some places."

Marian looped her arm through Kaitlin's, and

they walked together along the path. "What has you so quiet?" She nudged her with her shoulder. "Are you thinking about the Earl of Shelby?"

"What?" she asked in a surprised tone. "Of course not." Did Marian know Kaitlin loved him? No, that couldn't be it. She'd never voiced her feelings aloud with anyone, and she'd been as careful as possible to ensure no one suspected the truth. "I'm always quiet," Kaitlin answered.

"That is true," Marian agreed. Her tone suggested she didn't believe her though. "But something is different, and Shelby doesn't usually dance with anyone. It's strange he chose to at the Loxton ball. Do you think he plans on courting you?"

Kaitlin wasn't about to admit that she'd spent the entire trip to the Silverly picnic thinking about Shelby. She had hoped he'd be there, but didn't actually expect him to attend. The earl didn't often attend a social event unless he was required to. Most of the time, he left chaperoning Samantha to Marian since her marriage. Sometimes, though, he felt the need to make an appearance. Probably to remind the young bucks of his wishes regarding any courtship of his sister. He had to realize that at some point he would have to loosen his restrictions. Samantha deserved to find love and have a family of her own.

"He hasn't given me indication he wishes to do so. Shelby isn't the sort to allow anyone to be privy to his thoughts, and he often chooses to do things that baffles everyone." She shrugged. Marian was asking too many questions that she didn't wish to ponder too much over. She also didn't want to admit that the Earl of Shelby had essentially danced with her out of charity. "I've been considering my future." She had to tell Marian something. Kaitlin wasn't ready to admit she hoped Lord Shelby would be a part of that future.

"Have you made any decisions?"

Many and yet none…. "I haven't done well since our come out several years ago." She breathed a little easier now that it appeared Marian had given up interrogating her about the Earl of Shelby's decision to dance with her.

"That doesn't mean anything. You might still find love. I didn't believe I ever would."

"No," Kaitlin agreed. "The difference is you weren't looking. You wanted to be a doctor and didn't care if you ever married." Kaitlin had always craved a family. Uncle Charles and Marian had done their best, but she'd always felt as if something was missing. Her parent's death left a hole in her life, and she'd wanted to fill it with a family of her own.

"All that tells me is that you don't find love; it'll come to you when you least expect it." Marian smiled encouragingly.

"I agree." Because, up until that night at the Loxton ball, she'd been resigned to a life of spinsterhood. "And if I never have love, I'm all right with that." At least she'd find a way to accept the loss... "Now let's see what food they have for this picnic. I'm suddenly famished."

Marian dropped their topic of conversation, and they headed to the tents. Later she'd break away from her cousin and sit near the pond. She had a lot to think about, and it would be better if she did it alone.

GREGORY STARED AT ALL THE PEOPLE AT THE SILVERLY picnic and wondered why he'd agreed to attend with Samantha. He should find Harrington and ask him to look after her. He had to be at the picnic with his wife. With her expecting their first child, he wouldn't let her go alone, and Marian attended most social gatherings with her cousin, Lady Kaitlin Evans.

He hadn't been able to stop thinking about her.

Dancing with her had been a horrible idea. It put ideas inside his head he had been avoiding his entire adult life. She wasn't for him. Lady Kaitlin deserved someone with less tarnish on his soul. His was completely black and beyond redemption.

Still, he wanted to see her, and if she was at this blasted picnic he could. All he would have to do was locate her and strike a conversation. That shouldn't be too difficult.

Then why did the very idea of it terrify him?

Because she represented everything he secretly wished for but didn't believe he deserved. For that reason alone, he should keep his distance. If only she hadn't asked him to kiss her. He hadn't. Somehow, he had managed to keep his mouth off of hers, but it had been a close thing. He'd had his arms around her and her body flush against his. For a brief moment, he had even leaned in close enough to brush his lips against her soft golden hair.

He had wanted to kiss her. Do so much more than that but he hadn't. He regretted it too. Now all he wanted was to discover her whereabouts and press his lips against hers, then touch her until her moans of pleasure echoed around them.

He ran his hand through his hair as lust ravaged his body. He hardened at the thought of having her.

Gregory groaned at the idea of sinking his shaft deep into her welcoming softness. Bloody hell... He had to leave this picnic before he did something foolish. Maybe he should find a quiet place to get his body under control. He wasn't fit for polite society at the moment.

He scanned the area and saw a pond in the distance. A dip in its cold depths might be what he needed. He stalked toward it with purpose. It was far enough back and shrouded by trees to give him an element of privacy. It was a risk, but one he deemed worth it.

"Where are you going?" Samantha asked in a bewildered tone.

He stopped and pinned her with a hard gaze. "Don't you have friends you can bother instead of me?

"Well, I..." She glared at him. "What has you so testy?"

"Perhaps I've spent too much time in my sister's company. I've heard it drives a man to drink." He was being an arse and didn't care. He had to leave, and she was making it difficult for him.

"You are the one who is difficult. I'm the epitome of benevolence."

He snorted. "Sister dear, you really must stop

deluding yourself. You're nothing of the sort. What you are is a veritable shrew—a complete and utter hellion. It's best you accept it."

She squared her shoulders and her eyes filled with...hurt. He'd struck a blow he hadn't intended to. Gregory should apologize... He'd find time to do it later. It was always this way with them. He'd blunder and make it up to her later. His temper always found its way to the surface, and he'd have to make reparations.

That was why he didn't want a wife. He hated the idea of falling in love and hurting the one who held his heart. He wasn't a good man, and it would be inevitable he'd do something to cause a woman emotional agony of some sort. He'd blunder and act like an idiot. It was best he didn't get involved with a woman in that way or ever consider love an option for himself. Gregory couldn't find himself in that situation. It would gut him.

"If you're going to be surly, perhaps it is best you wander off. Marian is here with Kaitlin. I'll find them and have Marian act as my chaperone in your absence."

Kaitlin had arrived. He had to hold back the urge to search for her. If he saw her, he'd not be able to stop himself from heading in her direction. He had to go to that dratted pond and take a long soak in its cold depths. Maybe then he'd find a little relief from the heat that had become his constant companion since that waltz.

"I will be back," he told her. "Don't do anything foolish while I take a moment to myself."

"You have an assignation planned don't you," she accused.

He gritted his teeth. Gregory loved his sister, but he wanted to strangle her. "No," he said in a clipped tone. "Now run along and find Lady Harrington. Be a good girl for once and not the harpy you're known for."

She stomped her foot and clenched her fists, but she didn't say a word. Samantha spun on her heels and stormed away from him in a fit of rage. He didn't really blame her. In her place, he'd be angry with him too. He could have been nicer to her, but at the moment he didn't have it in him. Gregory shook his head and started toward the pond. Soon he would be immersed in its frigidness, and he'd finally be able to erase Lady Kaitlin Evans from his thoughts. At least he hoped so…

CHAPTER 6

*K*aitlin finally managed to pull herself away from Marian, and not a moment too soon… She'd caught a glimpse of Samantha heading in their direction before she'd slipped away. If she hadn't done so then she'd have been caught up in whatever drama Samantha had found herself in. Which meant she never would have found a moment alone at the pond.

She hadn't noticed the Earl of Shelby in attendance, but he had to be there somewhere. Samantha hadn't traveled with Marian and her, so that meant her brother had escorted her. A part of her wanted to seek him out, but she'd already had too much of the crowd. She needed the time away from them to breathe easier. There was only so much she could handle with social gatherings. She was not in her element at them, and much preferred staying home and reading. She'd stolen another one of Marian's medical texts and was a quarter of a way through it.

The closer she made it to the pond, the better she felt. Her stomach stopped clenching and her lungs filled with air without being on the verge of panic. No one ever came out to the pond. There was one reason to attend Lady Silverly's picnic and it wasn't the food. They came to see and be seen. This was one of the last gatherings of the season and there were still unattached young ladies in search of a husband. Kaitlin was presumably one of those ladies clamoring for a gentleman to offer for her. In some ways, she supposed she was, but she didn't want just any gentleman. Now that she decided to be brave enough to attempt for something more, only Lord Shelby would do for her. She hoped she hadn't pinned all her dreams on him to end up disappointed in the end.

The wind blew over her, pushing her bonnet off her head. The ribbon tied around her neck kept it from floating completely away. She kept walking toward the pond but stopped a moment to close her eyes and revel in the silence. A few more steps and she'd reach the tree near the pond's edge. She could sit under the large oak and enjoy the tranquility.

Kaitlin opened her eyes and headed toward her favorite resting spot. She had a place to hide at all the ton events. They always attended the same ones, and she found it helped her survive being thrown into the fray of society. As she drew closer, she discovered she wasn't as alone as she'd assumed. There were men's clothing hanging from a low branch. A pair of breeches, jacket, and waistcoat were neatly hung and blowing in the breeze. A white linen shirt had fallen to the ground over a pair of black Hessian boots.

Kaitlin brought her hand to her mouth, covering her shock. Somewhere near her was a very naked man, and she should run in the opposite direction, but she couldn't make her feet move. Her curiosity was getting the better of her. She'd never seen a naked man before. Something so scandalous would ruin her for sure. If she stayed, she'd catch sight of something that she'd only seen as a crude drawing in a medical journal. What would a naked man in the flesh resemble?

She really should stop reading Marian's medical books... Kaitlin nibbled on her lower lip and considered her options. Trust a rogue to dare to swim naked in a pond a short distance from one of the foremost prestigious social gatherings of the season. There wasn't another person that would dare risk it. As far as she was aware, one rogue of that caliber had deigned to attend the Silverly picnic.

The Earl of Shelby...

He must be the gentleman swimming, and she'd caught him *in flagrante delicto*. Well, not yet anyway. She hadn't spotted him in the pond, but she hadn't really looked either. It was time to rectify that mistake. Before, she'd been mildly curious about a male's naked body. Now that she believed it was Shelby, she *had* to find out if she was correct.

Kaitlin took several more steps, closing the distance between her and the pond. She narrowed her gaze in an attempt to bring the swimmer into focus. He, and she still assumed he was male, swam alone. She was grateful for that too. Kaitlin would have hated to interrupt a tryst of some sort. How scandalous would it be to swim naked with a man? She shivered at the idea. If it was with Shelby she'd be tempted to take a dip in the cold pond with him.

A ripple of waves traveled to the edge as a man swam toward her. He'd be upon her soon, and then she'd discover his identity. She prayed it was Shelby. If it was another man, she'd have a dilemma on her hands. She didn't want to be forced to marry a man she didn't love. He'd taken a risk swimming in the pond at the Silverly picnic. Kaitlin thought it was Shelby, and she couldn't help being excited at seeing some of his unclothed body. It was so scandalous to view him in that state. If he could take a risk, then so could she... She took a deep breath and waited for him to come forward.

As he swam closer, she decided to move backward. She didn't want him to notice her straightaway. Kaitlin wanted to observe him unencumbered first. As soon as he realized he wasn't alone, he'd act differently. She wanted him to be himself, so she could see who he was in private. It was wrong of her to sneak a peek at him, but if he was worried about it, he would not have swam naked in a public fashion. She refused to feel guilty about it.

He neared the edge of the pond and stood up, the water stopping just above his waist. He brushed his wet hair back with a sweep of his hand over the dark locks. The muscles in his biceps were well defined and bulging. His chest was magnificent and quite toned. Her gaze traveled down his belly and the dusting of hair near his navel. She licked her lips as she studied his gorgeous physique.

Had a more perfect male ever existed?

She didn't think so, but then she gazed upon him through the rose-tinted lens of love. Kaitlin had always found him to be perfect, and thus far she hadn't changed her mind.

"What the bloody hell are you doing here?"

Ah, he had noticed her finally. He must realize the mistake he'd made of swimming naked. Did he regret his choice? Should she leave him to dress in private? Kaitlin lifted a haughty brow. "It's a picnic, my lord. The question should be what made you decide to create a scandal?"

He flinched at her words, but she would not make it easy for him. As much as it pained her to be forward with him, it had to be this way. Shelby wouldn't want a meek wallflower for a wife. He'd want a lady that could stand up to him, and Kaitlin wanted him. She could fight for something if need be, but she preferred not to stand out. For Shelby though, she'd find courage where she needed to.

SHELBY CURSED UNDER HIS BREATH. HOW HAD HE ended up in this predicament? He narrowed his gaze. She was the reason he'd decided to take a swim in the cold pond. What was it about her that he suddenly found appealing? She was pretty enough, and she had gorgeous golden blonde hair. Lady Kaitlin was a tiny thing and didn't quite reach his shoulders. That fascinated him even more. Her small stature made her seem almost delicate.

None of which helped him discern the best solution to his current dilemma. He was not wearing a stitch of clothing and the object of his current obsession stood a few steps away from the edge of the pond. He could almost reach out and touch her. "Sweetheart," he flashed her his most wicked smile. "If you hadn't decided to wait for me to swim over, there wouldn't be a scandal to be had."

She lifted a brow mocking him. "I always visit this pond when I visit Silverly." Kaitlin placed her hands on her hips and glared at him. "Never once have I found anyone swimming in the pond before. Ducks, yes. Gentlemen, certainly not."

She was adorable. Lecturing him as if he were a small boy that deserved to have his ears boxed. Well, he probably did, but that's the last thing he wanted her to do with her hands. If his current quandary hadn't left him chest deep in the pond, he'd pull her into his arms and give her an entirely different sort of tongue lashing. "I'd step out of the pond, but I'd hate to make you blush." He rolled his gaze over her from top to bottom. "Though you do look pretty with your cheeks tinged pink. It gives a scoundrel like me ideas."

Maybe, if he embarrassed her, she'd scamper off. Lady Kaitlin wasn't known for having a stubborn streak. She wasn't meek by any means, but she usually remained passive. He understood why, considering she was a friend of his sister's. Samantha had an overbearing personality.

She laughed. It was a rich throaty chuckle that sent shivers down his spine. Kaitlin lifted her hand up to her mouth and stifled the laughter, then waved her hand as if trying to get control of it and failing. She stopped briefly and glanced back at him. "You expect me to think..." She started laughing again. "That *I* give you wicked ideas? Me? The wallflower no one notices?" She certainly found that idea hilarious.

Gregory scowled. "You don't believe I'd find you desirable?" Was she playacting, or did she truly believe that? "Perhaps your right." If she wanted to push him, he'd use that against her.

"Of course I am." She wiped a tear from the corner of her eye. "Now that we've settled that, I should leave you to..." She waved her hand.

"Whatever it is you're doing. Well, besides swimming."

"But what about the scandal?"

"There is no scandal if I leave," she insisted.

"No," he disagreed. "It's not that simple. What if someone sees you return and then me shortly after you do. They'll think the worst." He wouldn't allow that to happen to her. Gregory would slip away from the picnic altogether first, but she wouldn't know that.

"Drat," she said and then frowned. Kaitlin's shoulders slumped, and she glanced back toward the picnic. "Why do you have to be right?" She sighed. "What do you suggest we do then?"

He lifted his lips slowly. She might end up quite angry with him, but that was a risk he was willing to take. "Come closer, and I will tell you my plan."

She took several steps until she was at the edge of the pond. *Foolish girl...* He reached out and yanked her feet out from under her, and she landed in the pond with a loud splash. She leapt upward, her arms flailing around her. Gregory pulled her into his arms and tightened his embrace. She lifted her arms and looped them around his neck. "Why did you do that?"

"So I could save you," he replied nonchalantly.

"I didn't need anyone to save me." She lowered one of her hands and pushed him. "Let me go."

"I don't think so, sprite," he said huskily. "You wanted to taunt me, and now I believe it is my turn to return the favor."

"You're being ridiculous." Her voice lowered a little as she spoke, "I wasn't doing anything of the sort."

She could protest all she wanted, but he didn't think she was being honest, at least not with herself. He lowered his hands until they circled her waist. "You wanted to come for a swim with me, but didn't have the courage to jump in yourself. Admit it."

"You are wrong." She licked her lips.

His little sprite wanted him to kiss her. She'd asked him to at the ball, and he'd denied her then. Now that he had her in his arms, he couldn't stop himself from lowering his head. His lips were so close to hers they almost touched. "I'm never wrong," he said. "And I'm going to give you exactly what you asked for." Gregory pressed his lips to hers and lost all ability to think straight. He pushed his tongue inside her mouth and tasted her.

He'd never imagined heaven could be found in a kiss, but with Kaitlin he believed he'd found something close to salvation. She was sweet and tender, and he wanted to claim her. That was the dash of cold water he needed to stop. As wonderful as the kiss was, he had to put her first. She deserved far better than him, and he'd already gone farther than he ever should have. He pulled away and lifted her on the water's edge. "Go," he commanded. "Now."

"But…"

"Please don't argue with me." He clenched his teeth together. "This never should have happened."

She looked as if she might cry but did as he asked. She stood and slowly walked away from him. When she was far enough away, he got out of the pond and dressed. Then slipped away from the picnic and the temptation that was Lady Kaitlin Evans.

CHAPTER 7

Kaitlin stared out the window. It had been over a sennight since Lord Shelby had pulled her into the pond at the Silverly picnic. He hadn't tried to pay a call on her or anything resembling an apology. She couldn't recall a time that had been as embarrassing as that moment. After he'd ensured she would fall into the pond, he'd wrapped her in his embrace, while being stark naked, and kissed her until her mind turned to mush.

It had been wonderful, at least until the moment he'd destroyed her and any hope she might have. As she walked back to the picnic with her head held down in shame, she'd made a decision. The Earl of

Shelby wasn't ever going to love her. His kiss hadn't been one stemmed from desire, but one meant to punish her. It was time to move on and accept her life as a spinster.

"Katie," a young male shouted.

She turned and smiled at her little brother. Collin had grown while he was away. He'd just turned fifteen and was home from Eton for the summer. Kaitlin hugged him and then stepped back. She ruffled his strawberry blond hair and asked, "Did Uncle Charles bring you?"

He nodded enthusiastically. "He said Marian is planning a house party."

"She is?" Kaitlin lifted a brow. Her cousin hadn't mentioned that to her. She would have to locate Marian later and have a discussion. If possible, she'd like to avoid having her invite the Earl of Shelby. She wasn't hiding from him, but she would prefer not to see him yet. Her anger toward him hadn't simmered down enough to have a reasonable conversation with him.

"I get to stay for it," he said excitedly. "I never get to attend a party. What happens at them anyway? No one tells me anything."

She laughed. He had so much to learn.

Sometimes, she wondered if she was ever as young as her little brother. His innocence was enlightening. He'd been four years old when their parents had died and barely remembered them. Kaitlin was five years older than him and had been inconsolable. Now at twenty, she felt older than her years. "Then you're in for a treat. A house party lasts at least a sennight. Did Uncle Charles happen to tell you how long Marian has planned hers for?"

He shook his head. His blue eyes were bright with excitement. "No, but I hope it is an extra long one."

Kaitlin wanted the exact opposite as her brother. She wouldn't tell him that though. She liked that he was happy and wanted to ensure he stayed that way. If her brother had even a moment of sadness, it irritated her. They had both been through too much at a young age. She'd like to shelter her brother for as long as she could. "Well, then you'll have to help Marian plan her party. Why don't we go find her?"

Her little brother wasn't quite so little anymore. He was already much taller than her. Not that it took a lot for anyone to be, considering Kaitlin's short stature. In a couple years, Collin would be done with Eton and then continue his studies at Oxford. He'd probably take charge of the Frossly estate before then. At least he had their Uncle Charles to guide him. Marian's husband would be an asset as well. It was a large responsibility to be in charge of an earldom. In that, she didn't envy her little brother.

They exited the library and walked in silence to the sitting room that Marian liked to work out of while running the Harrington household. They found her studying a journal of some sort and not planning this house party Collin was so excited about.

"Is that a new medical journal?"

She glanced up and frowned. "It is. The Duchess of Weston sent it over for me to study."

The duchess was a female doctor that agreed to tutor Marian. "Is it helpful?" Collin asked as he stepped closer. "Can I look at it?"

Marian closed the book and set it aside. "Perhaps after I've finished, and with the duchess's permission, I could allow that." She smiled at Collin. "How are you doing? Did you learn a lot at school?"

He grinned. "It's nice to be home and not have everyone refer to me as Lord Frossly." He scrunched his nose up. "It's so...formal. I understand I have a place in society and being an earl is important, but..."

"You don't know who likes you for you," Marian said softly.

"I suppose that is true." He took a deep breath. "I will be glad when I'm done with school. It's not always a fun place to be." Collin lifted his lips. "Is it true you're planning a house party."

"Planned," she said. "The invitations have all been sent. We expect guests to start arriving as soon as today."

Kaitlin flinched. That meant there was a good chance Lord Shelby would be in attendance. "Is Samantha coming?" Her brother would have to escort her if she planned on being there for the gathering.

"I hope so," Marian answered her. "It wouldn't be the same without her. Though from her last missive, I'm not certain. She said Shelby has been acting odd."

She would not respond sarcastically to that bit of news. It would lead to questions she didn't particularly want to answer. It was bad enough she'd already had to endure an inquisition for having to leave the Silverly picnic early. Marian had not been able to understand how Kaitlin had fallen into the pond, but had been grateful she'd survived the ordeal, so hadn't pushed too much.

"If Samantha wants to attend, she'll find a way," Kaitlin said. "Nothing will stop her from doing whatever she wants, especially her brother." Shelby was probably just trying to prevent Samantha from meeting any new suitors. One day he'd have to allow his sister to settle down and find a husband. Kaitlin doubted he was acting any differently than usual.

Marian grinned. "Which is why I had a room prepared for her. I expect that she'd leave without Shelby and make him chase after her."

Sometimes she truly envied her friend. Kaitlin didn't think she could ever be that brave. She'd had a few moments with Lord Shelby, but it hadn't gone as she'd hoped it would. "I'm going to rest for a while." She nodded at her brother. "Glad you're home. We'll talk more later." After that, she left them alone in the room. Collin would continue to try and persuade Marian to let him look at the journal, and Kaitlin needed to be alone—to think. She had to decide how she wanted to deal with Lord Shelby when he turned up at the estate. He had a lot to answer for.

BLOODY HELL... GREGORY COULDN'T PINPOINT WHEN

his life had taken a bad turn, but he wished he could go back and change it. He'd been making mistake after mistake for the past fortnight, probably longer. Ever since Lady Kaitlin Evans had asked him to kiss her. That was probably when it had all gone wrong. She'd had to make him notice her, and once he had he couldn't forget her. Now his sister was determined to make him atone for his sins whether she realized it or not.

Samantha had her trunks packed, loaded on the back of a carriage, and rolling down the road before he could stop her. He'd had to scramble to catch up to her. The grooms seemed to take forever to saddle his horse so he could head to Harrington's estate. It was the one place she'd defy him to go to. The two ladies she was closest to were already there. That was the very reason he'd been dead set against going.

He didn't want to face Kaitlin. If he could go the rest of his life and not see her again... No, he couldn't do that either. The idea of never setting his gaze upon her lovely face again seemed wrong. Gregory wished he had made a different choice. There was one problem with being near Kaitlin again.

He would have to apologize. Gregory hated going through the motions of saying he was sorry. It never felt good. Especially since most of the time he had no remorse and he didn't bother making excuses. For all his faults, he owned every one of them.

At least his friend's estate wasn't too far from London. He'd only had to stop to rest his horse once. After a couple hours at an inn and a hot meal in his belly he'd taken off again. He should be arriving at the Earl of Harrington's estate soon. Samantha would already be there. When he located her, he'd pull her aside and chastise her for disregarding his wishes. They'd have a row again. It seemed as if they always fought whenever they crossed paths. The Cain temper reared its ugly head more often than not, and Samantha knew how to rile him more than anyone.

The estate came into view, and he motioned for his horse to turn down the long winding drive. He slowed to a trot as he approached the main entrance. When he reached it, he hopped down and handed the reins to a waiting groomsman. With the estate in the throes of a house party, they were prepared for any and all arrivals. "Have someone take my valise to whatever room I'm assigned to." Lady Marian would have prepared for his arrival when Samantha had appeared.

He skipped the steps two at a time and strolled into the house. Gregory had been to Harrington's estate several times and was familiar with the layout. He planned on heading straight to Harrington's library and helping himself to his expensive brandy. A drink sounded like a piece of heaven and something he desperately needed. He strolled down the hall with even strides and went directly into the library.

Gregory poured two fingers of brandy and lifted the glass to his mouth and froze in place. His focus had been entirely on the shelf with liquor, so he didn't notice the room's other occupant until that moment. Lady Kaitlin lounged on the window seat in the library, her attention engrossed on the book in her lap. Sun streamed down on her, making her golden hair glow. It almost appeared as if she had a halo. He didn't want to disturb her, but the urge to speak to her was too great.

"That must be riveting," he said in a droll tone. It was his attempt to keep the situation light. Maybe she wasn't mad at him, but he somehow doubted she'd forgive him so easily. In her place, Gregory wouldn't have absolved him. He'd ordered her to leave him and walk back into a social gathering, dripping wet. That had to have been be awful for her.

She glanced up and glared at him. "Much more entertaining than your company." Kaitlin closed the book with a *thud*. "I'll leave you to your drink."

He was...disappointed. Gregory had expected more vehemence and fury from her. "The brandy has some fire in it." He took a sip and let it slide down his throat. "That's more than you're capable of." It was perhaps not his finest moment. Goading her would not solve anything, but he couldn't stop himself.

She spun on her heels and stormed over to him. Before he could stop her, she snatched the glass from his hand. He thought perhaps she intended to throw the drink in his face, but she didn't. Instead, she swallowed the contents whole and smiled wantonly at him. "You're right," she said. Her voice had an intensity he hadn't noticed from her before. "It has a nice burn to it, but it's special in an entirely different way."

"How's that?" he asked, curiosity getting the better of him.

She set the glass down hard on a nearby table. Then glanced at him without flinching. Kaitlin licked her lips as if savoring the remnants of the brandy. "I wouldn't mind having it roll across my tongue again. That headiness that flowed over my lips...pure pleasure." She stepped a little closer and trailed her fingers over his chest. "That's something I can't say I've experienced with you." With those words, she spun around and left him alone in the library...speechless.

CHAPTER 8

The afternoon sun streamed down over Kaitlin as she strolled through the back lawn. She hoped she wouldn't cross paths with Shelby. She didn't want to share any more barbs with him. He'd barely been at the house party a day, and he was already driving her mad. At least he'd skipped dinner and she hadn't been required to endure his company through the meal. She might not have been able to keep any food in her belly. Now it was the next day, and she had a feeling he'd make an appearance, and in turn, do his damn best to cause her some sort of misery.

Servants were in the far back lawn of the Harrington estate, setting up several tents and preparing for the activities planned over the course of the house party. Marian had a lot of different games and sporting events prearranged for the entire fortnight. Kaitlin admired her cousin's ability to organize everything and still find time to study her medical texts. Sometimes she wondered where her cousin found the motivation to do it all.

She strolled along the perimeter in an attempt to stay out of the servants' paths. Kaitlin didn't want to be a nuisance. A footman stepped in front of her, carrying a large wooden box filled with equipment of some sort. She tripped over her own feet in an attempt to avoid colliding with him. Someone steadied her from behind.

"Thank you," she said as she attempted to catch her breath.

"Think nothing of it," a male said. She glanced up and met the Earl of Asthey's gaze. He was a handsome man with golden blond hair and ice blue eyes. "Anyone would have given you aid if they were in my place."

"It was still kind of you to prevent my fall, so you have my gratitude regardless." Why couldn't Lord Shelby be this polite with her? He had been a complete arse in the library when he'd arrived. "My cousin has a lot of entertainments planned. Are you looking forward to a particular one?" She scrunched her eyebrows together. "I'm not certain what that servant is carrying." Kaitlin gestured toward a man that had long paddle-looking items in his arms. "Are they for a boat?"

He chuckled softly. "I'm afraid not. Those are bats for cricket. I trust you've never seen a match?"

"I can't say that I have." She shook her head. "I have been told it's quite amusing."

"I prefer shooting to games of this sort, but I frequently played cricket when I attended Eton. It's not a difficult game." Asthey gestured toward the paddles. "Will you play when they set up a game?"

"Considering I don't know much about cricket, it's probably best that I don't embarrass myself by trying." Kaitlin hated having any attention on her. She'd much rather sit on the sidelines. It was much safer there. She could clap and cheer everyone on. She wasn't sure how vocal she'd actually be. She'd probably slide into the shadows and observe everyone in silence. Lord Asthey didn't need to know any of that though. "Will you play?"

"Most likely," he replied. "Harrington and Shelby like to wager on the game. They'll get Darcy here too. The four of us will split between the two teams and the victors will demand a boon of some sort."

"Really?" she lifted a brow. That was interesting.

"You have played this in the past? What type of boon is usually required?"

Asthey opened and closed his mouth several times. The earl was probably trying to ascertain the best way to reply to her inquiry. After a few moments he started to speak. "I wish I could impart details on our past wagers, but I'm afraid it would be irresponsible of me to deliver such information to an innocent lady."

Of course he wouldn't tell her. If she were being honest with herself, she never expected him to. Gentlemen have long made wagers and pursued wild activities. Their boons probably had something to do with drinking or loose women. Perhaps all of it combined. "Lord Shelby is already here. Do you expect Lord Darcy to arrive soon?"

Most of the guests were already in attendance, but Marian had mentioned at breakfast that there were still a few that expected to arrive later in the day. Lord and Lady Darcy were probably in the late stragglers.

"It's my understanding that he's traveling from his sister's. Darcy and his wife are a distance away from here, but I suppose they all should be here today." He nodded toward the many tents and the servants. "If you wish to learn how to play cricket,

I'd be willing to teach you. We're not having a match until tomorrow the earliest. Most of the equipment will be stored in the tents until we're ready to play."

She nibbled on her bottom lip and considered his offer. Did she really wish to play the game? It might be interesting to learn, and if she wished to experience a game of cricket she'd be armed with the necessary skills. "I…" She swallowed hard. "I don't do well with social activities."

He tilted his head to the side and seemed to consider her confession. Lord Asthey smiled. "Come walk with me a bit." He held out his arm to her. "I'll tell you a bit about myself, and perhaps that will put you at ease."

Kaitlin placed her arm through his and they strolled along the lawn. The servants that they crossed paths with dodged them with skill Kaitlin admired. He led her to one of the tents and they ducked inside. The earl let go of her arm and went over to one of the wooden crates. He pulled out a bat and held the handle end out to her. "Go ahead, take it."

She reached tentatively for it. "What do you expect me to do with this?"

"Hold it for the moment." He reached down and grabbed a second one. "When I was a boy at Eton, a day didn't go by that I wasn't teased in some fashion. When I was younger, I was quite sickly. Activity of any kind was a strain on my health. There were times my family believed I'd not grow to adulthood."

"And they sent you away to school?" That was horrible. They should have kept him at home if he took sick so often. "Why would they do that?"

"Because all boys of good breeding went to an exemplary school. My father chose to send me to Eton instead of Harrow like he'd attended. I suspect because he was embarrassed by his weakling of a son," Asthey explained. "I'll never know for sure and I've digressed a little. There is a reason for me to explain all of this."

"There is?" It was a rather personal story. "Why do you think I should know all of this?"

"Because you said you don't do well in social situations. I wanted you to understand I haven't always been able to immerse myself in a crowd. Even today I prefer my own company. My friends are the reason I bother with social niceties." He smiled. "Cricket helped me acclimate in ways I never would have imagined. I'll never love the game, but I do remember it fondly. Shelby is the one who nearly dragged me out on to the field kicking and screaming."

"Somehow, that doesn't surprise me." Lord Shelby had audacity in spades. He did whatever he wanted, and to hell with the consequences. She learned that lesson about him the hard way. "Is that how you became friends."

"Oh, we weren't friends at first." His smile widened into a grin. "I hated him, and when I was forced in front of the bowler and had to hit the ball for the first time, I imagined it was his head."

The more he talked, her interest in learning to play cricket increased. "I think I understand why you're telling me this now. Cricket is a way to take out my aggravations without harming anyone." She tilted her head to the side. "You've convinced me. Show me how to hold this thing properly."

Asthey chuckled, raised the bat in the air, and then began her cricket lessons. He probably wouldn't appreciate the fact she intended to imagine Shelby's face when they started the next step of her lessons and she practiced hitting the ball. It was rather funny in a way that he'd done the same all those years ago...

Gregory wandered around the house in search

of Asthey. He ducked into the library and perused the room quickly and ascertained it was empty. He stepped out and stopped short as his sister approached him. "There you are," she said. "I wish to discuss something with you."

"Not now," he told her and brushed past her.

"Yes now," she said petulantly and fell in step beside him. "This has to stop." Samantha reached out and placed her hand on his arm. "Gregory," she said softly. "Please."

He had to find a way to evade this conversation. His sister rarely used his given name, and each time she'd done so hadn't ended well for him. She wanted something from him, and he had a feeling he wouldn't like it. Gregory stopped and let out a long breath. "I presume from your tone that whatever you have to discuss with me is important—at least to you." Samantha wouldn't allow him to delay the conversation. Not easily anyway… "But I really don't have time at the moment. I have been tasked to find Lord Asthey, and he seems to have disappeared."

Samantha narrowed her gaze. "You're searching for Lord Asthey?"

Gregory's patience was running thin. "I am," he answered a bit tersely.

"If I were to assist you in locating him, then

would you have a moment to spare me?" She lifted a brow questioningly, but her tone was curt. "I mean, if that wouldn't be too much trouble for my busy brother."

Clearly, he'd been neglecting his sister's needs. Whatever those were... He'd have to rectify that oversight, and he was fairly certain she wouldn't be happy about it when he did so. "Are you aware of Lord Asthey's current location?"

"And if I am?"

Gregory cursed under his breath. "Would you be so kind as to impart your knowledge regarding Lord Asthey so I may go to his current location and have a much-needed conversation with him."

"You mean like the one I wish to have with you?" Samantha asked.

He'd had enough of Samantha's stalling tactics. Gregory could continue his search without her assistance. He took a step in the opposite direction of his sister and headed toward the back of the estate. "Wait," she called out and ran to catch up to him. "We can talk while we look."

"You implied you were aware where to find him," he accused her. "Were you lying to me to somehow gain the upper hand?" Gregory was already on edge. A certain female had put him firmly in a foul mood by denying she'd enjoyed his kiss. Nothing would convince him she hadn't found it pleasurable. The affronted side of him wanted to kiss her again and prove her wrong. To show her that she hadn't been truthful. While the end of their little tête-à-tête hadn't been the best up until its fateful ending, nothing but pleasure had been shared between him and Kaitlin. He wouldn't allow Kaitlin's barb to bait him then, and he would not let his sister lead him astray now.

"I wasn't lying," she answered. "I do know where he is, but I didn't want you to disturb them."

"Them?" He tilted his head to the side. "Pray tell, who is Lord Asthey with, and why would you feel the need to protect them?"

She shuffled her feet and glanced away. "You have this tendency to overreact, and Kaitlin..."

He saw red. Was his friend courting Lady Kaitlin? A sour taste filled his mouth at the idea of her with Asthey. She shouldn't be with him. Did she hope that Asthey would offer her marriage? Was he the man she hoped to gain attention from? Kaitlin belonged... He shook that thought away before it could fully form. "Asthey showed interest in her before." He hated admitting that much. "Is this your blundering way of telling me he's resumed the idea of courting her?"

"I couldn't say for certain," she began. She tilted her head to the side and adopted a feigned look of innocence. It was ruined when her mouth twitched a little, and she attempted to hide her amusement. What the bloody hell did she find so entertaining? She tapped her chin lightly with her forefinger as if pondering a thought. "But I did notice him teaching her how to swing a bat for cricket. The servants are setting up some of the events for tomorrow."

Cricket. The entire reason he was searching for his friend. They had to decide on the teams. Harrington had sent him to retrieve Asthey so they could organize it. "Kaitlin isn't thinking of playing, is she?" He wouldn't allow it. She could get hurt. Gregory didn't give his sister a chance to answer the question. He spun on his heels and headed to where the cricket game would be played. When he found them, he'd knock some sense into his friend and chastise Kaitlin for her foolish behavior.

CHAPTER 9

*G*regory stomped across the field toward Asthey and Kaitlin. Asthey held a cricket bat up to her. She tentatively placed her hand on the handle and took it away from him. Neither one of them turned in his direction. Samantha trailed on his heels but was having trouble keeping up with his long strides.

"Wait," Samantha yelled. "You're going to ruin everything."

He certainly intended to. Gregory was going to stop it all before it had a chance to go any farther. What was Asthey thinking? He stalked forward, closing the remaining distance between them, and Kaitlin turned to face Gregory. She extended her arm straight with the end of the bat reaching his chin, making him immediately halt. Almost like someone brandishing their fencing foil and begging them to concede defeat. "Don't take another step," Kaitlin ordered. "I've learned a little how to use this, and I wouldn't mind some practice on a larger target."

She'd threatened him. Sweet, innocent, and often shy Kaitlin held a bat at his throat and was attempting to browbeat him, force him to bend to her will. Gregory might be a little sadistic, but he found it a little arousing. He'd be damn proud of her if he weren't the target of her wrath. What the hell was wrong with him? He liked her even more for not being intimidated by him.

Samantha finally caught up with him. She reached out and placed her hand on the extended bat and lowered it from Gregory's chin. "I understand the sentiment, but let's not give in to our first impulse. My brother is difficult to deal with, but I doubt beating some sense into him will help much. He's rather stubborn, and it won't register in his thick skull what he's done wrong."

"I resent that," Gregory replied mulishly. "I've done nothing wrong." Besides, he could be reasonable. Samantha's description made him seem like an errant child.

Kaitlin's lips tilted upward. She was beautiful, but that smile made him a little uneasy. "I'm aware of his faults. More than I'd like to admit."

"Then you'll go easy on him. He is my brother, so I'd rather not see him dead even if sometimes he might deserve it." Samantha's smile matched Kaitlin's. The females of his acquaintance were ganging up on him. Samantha gestured toward the bat that Kaitlin still held. "How are your lessons on how to play cricket going? Do you hope to play tomorrow?"

"She's not playing," Gregory insisted. Asthey laughed. Gregory might yet hit his friend. "Why would you teach her?"

He shrugged. "It seemed harmless enough."

Showed what his friend knew. "Harrington won't allow it. If we let her play, then all the females will want to. If his wife gets the idea in her head to join in, he'll have a fit. She's *enceinte*."

"Marian won't put her baby at risk," Samantha said. "You have no faith in a woman's ability to make rational decisions." She shook her head and stared at him as if she were disappointed in him. It wouldn't be the first time. He often frustrated his sister.

He ignored his sister's remark. It was rare a woman acted sensibly, and he stood by his earlier words. Lady Harrington wanted to be a physician and had gone to extreme lengths to achieve that goal. Her actions proved that she could and would insist upon doing something that wouldn't necessarily be a wise decision. She might very well make a fine doctor, but it was still dangerous for her nonetheless. Gregory believed Harrington was far too complacent with her predilections. He turned his attention to Asthey. "Are you done with your cricket lessons?"

"I was about to take her out and bowl the ball to her a few times. She finally has an understanding of a proper swing."

Gregory raised his hand and pinched the bridge of his nose. He prayed for patience, but was failing to keep his anger under control. "I cannot believe we're actually discussing having her attempt to hit a ball that is bowled to her. Why would you consider it?"

"Because its fun?" Asthey suggested. "Or liberating?"

"I think it's a fantastic idea," Samantha said. "We should have a bit of a game." She turned to Kaitlin. "Do you wish to make it more interesting? You've been quiet for a while now. I know you don't like confrontations, and my brother is being ridiculous."

"I'm all right," Kaitlin said. "And I believe a game would be fun, but don't we need more players? I thought each team had eleven. There are four of us, and we're quite a few people short to make even one team, let alone two."

"It wouldn't be a true game," Samantha said and waved her hand dismissively."

"It won't be a game at all," Gregory interrupted her. "We're not doing it."

"I suppose you don't have to play if you don't wish to, but it would be boring if you didn't." Samantha turned to Asthey and smiled. "You'll join us, won't you?"

Asthey lifted his hand and placed his thumb and forefinger under his chin as he considered her question. "You're right, Lady Kaitlin," he began. "We can't play a traditional game, but we could make do. In two teams of two, we could have a bowler and a fielder on one side, and a batsman and runner on the other."

"The wickets are already set up," Samantha said, gesturing to the two sets of three stumps with two bails placed on top of each. She turned toward Gregory. "Please say you'll join us. We can either group by gender or one male, one female on each team."

Gregory had to be insane for considering this. "Fine." Maybe he could find a way to talk to Kaitlin while he participated in this farce. "We should split evenly. One male and one female per team."

"Perfect," Samantha said. "I'll be on your team, and Kaitlin can be with Lord Asthey."

He glared at his sister. That wasn't how he wanted it to go at all. Gregory gritted his teeth and smiled or at least tried to. He was afraid it very much looked like a snarl. "I'll bowl. You can field." He motioned for Samantha to take her position then turned to Kaitlin and Asthey. "Which one of you will be the batsman and runner?"

Kaitlin held up her bat. "I'd like to try this out."

Asthey nodded. "Works for me." He jogged out into place to run when needed. Kaitlin took her place in front of the wicket. Gregory picked up a leather-bound ball and advanced toward the opposite wicket and then stood in front of it. He held his arm out straight and wound up to bowl the ball to her. The ball went flying, and she hit it with a resounding *smack* echoing around them. Gregory wasn't prepared for her to actually make contact or the ball hitting him directly in the face. He fell backward hitting the ground with a *thud*.

KAITLIN PACED HER ROOM, STILL SHOCKED SHE'D NOT only hit the ball that hard, but managed to direct it at Lord Shelby. Guilt had spread through her immediately. He hadn't bothered to even look at her. After he'd picked himself up off the ground, he stormed off. She wanted to make sure he was all right, but allowed her fear to sway her otherwise.

A knock echoed through the room. She nibbled on her bottom lip and then sighed. Kaitlin didn't know who could be visiting her, but she didn't believe it was good. She went to the door and opened it. Samantha was on the other side. "Is he all right?"

"He's fine," she reassured her. "He has a hard head. I believe I mentioned that earlier. It's my fault really. I shouldn't have suggested we play in the first place."

"We didn't get very far, but it did feel good to hit that ball." She grinned, and then her smile fell fast. "At least until I realized where the ball landed."

Samantha went to a chair and sat down. "I think there is much more going on between you and my brother than I realized. It didn't occur to me until afterward, but he was acting strangely. The only time he gets that protective is with me. I should have seen it sooner." She nibbled on her lower lip. "The dance. That's were it began. My brother never deigns to dance at a ball. How could I have not discerned the truth before now?" She tilted her head to the side and had a thoughtful expression on her face.

"I'm not certain I understand what you're implying." Lord Shelby, in her opinion, acted exactly as she had come to expect. Brutish, condescending, and domineering...

"He's in love with you." That was Samantha—guileless and right to the point.

Her heart skipped a beat at Samantha's words. For a brief moment, she allowed herself to accept the possibility Samantha might be right. Kaitlin would like to believe she spoke the truth. That her brother did love her, but she couldn't... "I very much doubt that." Lord Shelby had never done anything that would lead her to believe he loved her. One kiss and a dance... That meant nothing. She certainly had hoped that he would come to care for her. Had even dreamed his attention might lead them to that point, but had given up on the idea after that unfortunate incident in the pond at Lady Silverly's picnic.

"Please sit," Samantha gestured toward a nearby chair.

Kaitlin did as she suggested but didn't want to continue their current conversation. She was glad that Lord Shelby was all right, but Samantha was correct. "I'm not going to change my mind. Your brother is a lot of things, but a man smitten is not one of them."

Samantha was quiet for a moment. When she started to speak, her voice was soft. "When we first met, we seemed like two different people. I can be a bit of a hellion, and with that comes a demanding personality."

"And I appear shy and demure because I prefer to observe than participate in a conversation," Kaitlin finished.

"But as we began to talk and share with each other we discovered we had far more in common than we would have realized looking on the surface." Samantha placed her hand on Kaitlin's. "We both lost our mothers at a young age. I barely remember mine, but you have wonderful memories of yours. Gregory..." She took a deep breath. "Our mother's death scarred him. Our father didn't handle her death well, and for a while he went wild. I'm not certain what helped him straighten out and decide to be more of a father to us, but the damage was already done. In some ways, we had lost both of our parents, and my brother never fully recovered."

Kaitlin could understand that. She still keenly felt the loss of her parents. "So, his horrible demeanor is because he grew up without his mother?" She raised her eyebrow. "You're right, I do feel a bit of empathy for your loss, and yes, your brothers. How could I not? That doesn't mean I will excuse his behavior. He's acted abysmally toward me, and I deserve better than that."

"I don't disagree." She sighed. "But I had hoped you'd take pity on him. He won't admit how he feels because he doesn't believe he warrants any happiness."

Kaitlin wanted to believe her. The idea of Lord Shelby loving her...filled her with hope she had thought crushed already. She had been so angry with him. That rage had enabled her to keep her distance and treat him as if he'd meant nothing to her. His dismissal of her had bruised her heart and her barely-there confidence. It took a lot for her to open herself up to anyone. "What do you expect me to do?"

"Push him," Samantha suggested. "Make him admit how he feels."

Kaitlin didn't think it would be that simple. "Are you already forgetting how stubborn your brother is? What do you think I could possibly do to encourage him to admit he may or may not love me?"

"Oh, he definitely loves you," Samantha insisted. "I believe you feel the same way about him. Otherwise, you wouldn't have been ready to smack him with the cricket bat." She smiled shamelessly. "Only my brother could inspire that much rage."

Kaitlin frowned. "When does anger equate love?" She'd thought she'd hid her feelings from everyone.

"It does when you add my brother into the mix. It's the one thing he responds well too. It's probably driving him insane that he loves you when he doesn't believe he can have you. Then you add in your little cricket lesson with Lord Asthey. It rankled him far more than he'd ever willingly admit. He doesn't want any other gentleman to pay you any attention, and he was going to ensure he put some distance between the two of you. Trust me. He feels deeply for you. My brother would go that far for someone he loves. It's why he's scared off every one of my suitors." She rolled her eyes. "Something I'm going to put a stop to at the first opportunity. It seemed endearing at first, but now it's absurd. How does that idiot expect me to find a husband, let alone love, when he keeps blocking the possibility of either one?"

"I doubt he's thought that far ahead," Kaitlin said sympathetically. "He is trying to protect you."

"I don't need him to," Samantha said vehemently. "I admit I have an ulterior motive in trying to match you with my brother."

"You're not trying to bring two people together that you believe love each other out of the goodness of your heart?" Kaitlin batted her eyelashes together. "Then what is it you do want?"

"A female with influence over my difficult brother." She smiled mischievously. "Do you think you are up for the task?"

Kaitlin wasn't certain she could convince Lord Shelby of anything, but she did want to discover if they did have something between them. If Samantha believed it, then Kaitlin owed it to herself to find out if it was true. If Lord Shelby did love her, they might have a chance at real happiness. "All right," she finally said. "I'll speak to him, but I'm not making any promises."

"That's all I can ask," Samantha replied. "And I'll hope for a desirable outcome. I do want you both to be happy."

Kaitlin wanted that too. She wasn't confident in the possibility... She'd keep an open mind though and approach Lord Shelby carefully. She didn't want to poke the beast and end up with a completely shattered heart in the process.

CHAPTER 10

Gregory leaned his head back against the arm of the leather chaise he'd plopped down on in the library. His cheek below his eye bloody hell hurt. He lifted his hand and pressed his fingers to the tender flesh and winced. Kaitlin had hit that ball as if she'd been playing cricket for years, and he'd managed to stand like an unflinching fool as if he'd never played a day in his life.

He needed a drink...probably several. The brandy was on the shelf behind him. It seemed so far away. If he wanted a glass, he'd have to find the motivation to move. The little drummers inside his head told him any sudden actions would result in even greater pain.

The echo of someone slow clapping filled the room. He glanced toward the entrance as Lord Darcy sauntered inside. Every strand of his blond hair was perfectly in place, and no wrinkles graced his dark gray traveling clothes. There had to be something wrong with a man who remained presentable after a long journey. "What the blazes are you making that racket for?" He glared at his friend.

"It's not for you," he explained. "Though your irritation by it is a nice side benefit."

"If you've come to gloat..." Crinkles formed around his blue eyes, making him appear quite amused at Gregory's predicament.

"Oh, I definitely have," Darcy interrupted him. "It's a wonderful sight to see you waylaid in a similar manner as I was almost a year ago. You do recall using your fists on my gorgeous face and marring it, do you not?" He turned his head from side to side. "Luckily, it wasn't permanent. My wife does prefer my more perfect visage." He walked over to the liquor and poured himself a glass of brandy. "Now seeing your pretty face turning that lovely shade of purple...couldn't have happened to a more deserving man." He sipped his brandy and then said, "My apologies, did you need a spot of your own?"

He closed his eyes and prayed for patience. Darcy was right, after all. Gregory had used his fists on him when the earl had attempted to court Samantha. He hadn't felt Darcy would make a good match for his sister, and he'd been right. "You were in love with someone else, and Samantha shouldn't live as any one's second choice. If you had been inclined to listen to reason, I wouldn't have had to pummel you at all." He opened his eyes and met Darcy's gaze. "And you better bloody hell pour me some of that brandy."

Darcy chuckled and did as Gregory demanded. He carried the full glass over to him. Gregory snatched it out of the earl's hands and swallowed half of it in one gulp. It burned down his throat, but he hoped the brandy's mind-disorienting effects would put him into a stupor as quick as possible.

"So tell me," Darcy began. He waved his finger in a circle around the welt on Gregory's face. "Who decided to give you that delightful mark of love? There are whispers that Lady Kaitlin Evans delivered the blow. Please tell me you didn't entice that sweet woman into violence."

"Would if I could," he replied. He took another long drink of his brandy. Darcy's assessment of Kaitlin was correct. She was indeed sweet and had never been prone to violence of any sort. In fact, she tended to avoid conflict of any kind. It took a closer acquaintance with him for her to develop a slow burning rage. He didn't blame her. Blame for the entire incident could be laid at his feet. He never should have touched her. Even if she had asked for him to kiss her...he should not have acted upon it. "I'm afraid I'm not fit for polite company."

"Bollocks," Darcy said in disagreement. "You are more than capable of acting like a perfect gentleman. The problem is you choose to act like an absolute arse." He sat down on a nearby chair. "Do you wish to know what I think?"

"No," Gregory said glibly, "but somehow, I do not believe that would stop you." He flicked his hand in a contemptuous manner. "Do continue so we can move away from this topic."

Darcy tapped his finger against his glass in a repetitive motion. "You love the girl."

Gregory mentally cursed. He really didn't want to have this conversation. He had to find a way to steer it in another direction. "You're wrong."

"Am I?" Darcy grinned. "Don't admit it. Be miserable for the rest of your life." He stood up and then lifted his glass to his mouth. Darcy drained the remaining brandy and set the empty cup on a nearby table. He faced Gregory and said, "Or you can tell her how you feel and attempt to find your own slice of happiness."

He walked to the door to exit the room, but stopped briefly to turn back and say. "Before I leave… Harrington has decided that you and I are to be on the same team at the cricket match. He believes we have some issues to work through and combining our skills will help achieve that goal. In addition, he muttered something about marriage and bachelorhood. I could be wrong, but he might believe with my marriage and his, we should prevail upon you and Asthey the benefits of the establishment."

Gregory snorted. "Harrington should mind his own business as should you."

"Have it your way," Darcy said. "You always do." With that, he exited the room, leaving Gregory alone.

He hadn't moved much since the earl had entered the library. It rankled that his friend had been right on every point he'd made. Gregory did love Lady Kaitlin. He wasn't even sure when it had happened. Somewhere along the way, his heart had decided she was the sole woman for him. The problem, of course, was Gregory didn't deserve her and he should keep his damn hands off of her. He also didn't, for a moment, believe himself capable of that particular feat.

KAITLIN STROLLED HESITANTLY TOWARD THE LIBRARY and stopped short of the entrance. A servant had informed her that Lord Shelby could be found there, but now she wasn't sure of the wisdom of her plan. She twisted her hands in front of her and shuffled her feet, then took a deep fortifying breath. The worst he could say was he didn't love her. Considering she had her doubts that he did, it should not be that difficult to accept. She continued inside and found him lying across a settee. Lord Shelby had a glass of brandy in his hand. He lifted it and set the glass against his forehead, then closed his eyes. He moaned, probably from pain. Guilt spread through her and she forced herself to continue toward him.

His eyelids fluttered open upon her approach. "Have you come to put me out of my misery?"

"No," she said softly. "I've come to apologize."

"You have nothing to be sorry for," he said gruffly. "Don't bother with self recriminations."

"Do you think it's that easy?" She shook her head. "It's not, and how I feel isn't going to disappear because you order it so." She hated that he dismissed her so easily. When he'd pulled her into the pond and kissed her senseless, he'd pushed her away after. During that kiss she'd thought, finally. Finally, he'll admit how much he needed her. There was something between them. He couldn't have kissed her so passionately if he didn't have any feelings for her. "Why do you believe I came in here to do you further harm?"

"Because I deserve it." He lowered his brandy and emptied the glass, then set it on the floor next to the settee. "If you doubt my earlier words, I honestly do not blame you. It was an accident."

"I know," she said. "I would never deliberately hurt you."

He remained quiet for a few moments. She stood there waiting for him to speak. Kaitlin hoped she wouldn't have to pull information out of him. More importantly, she wanted him to admit to her what made him keep himself at a distance. After that, they could move forward, and with any luck...together.

Lord Shelby met her gaze. "It was never my intention to hurt you, but somehow I have." His voice was filled with remorse.

Kaitlin took another step forward and tentatively reached out to touch the large bruise forming on his left cheek. "Does it pain you much?"

"Like the devil," he admitted. "Do you wish to make it all better?"

"If I could, I would," she told him. She hated that her actions resulted in such an angry injury.

"You can." He lifted his lips into a wicked smile. "Lean down and press your lips against it." He tapped his bruised cheek lightly with his forefinger. "I've heard a kiss can have magical properties."

She narrowed her gaze. "How much brandy have you imbibed?"

"Not nearly enough." He motioned toward the decanter on the shelf behind him. There was another empty glass there. "Darcy poured himself one and deigned to give me one as well. I haven't had the motivation to pour any more."

Kaitlin considered what he'd suggested. He was teasing, of course. Lord Shelby didn't believe for a moment that she'd actually go through with the task of kissing him. She was willing to wager he didn't think she'd be brave enough to take that risk. "Magical you say?" She tilted her head to the side. "That hasn't been my experience with kissing."

He groaned. "Please do *not* tell me that you didn't

find the kiss we shared pleasurable again. Haven't you bruised me enough today?"

Kaitlin was starting to see what Samantha had. Lord Shelby kept his emotions buried, but when he cared he did so deeply and completely. She still wasn't certain he loved her. His actions didn't inspire her to believe that much, but it was time to test Samantha's theory. If he loved her, and she had started to think it might be possible, then she'd have to find a way to encourage him to admit it.

"What made you storm out to the cricket field?" She took a step closer. "There was no danger. Lord Asthey was taking care of me and teaching me a new skill. I was grateful for the time and kindness he showed me."

"I'm sure he was a complete gentleman." There was bitterness in his tone.

"Is that wrong?" She lifted a brow. "There was a time you offered to help me find a husband. What if I decided Lord Asthey is the gentleman for me?"

He scowled. "And have you?"

There wasn't much space between them. She closed what little distance remained. Her legs were flush against the settee. All she had to do was lean down and press her lips softly against his cheek. After that, she believed he wouldn't be able to remain passive. There were other answers she needed first though. "I did have one gentleman in mind when you agreed to help me." What she didn't say was that it had always been him She loved him and only him. No one else would ever fill her heart the way he did. Even when he acted like a complete arse, she adored him.

He closed his eyes and let out a deep breath. "You should always have what you want. I…" He swallowed hard. "I don't know if I can persuade Asthey, but if that is your desire, I'll try."

"How noble of you," she said and smiled. Somehow, this man who had a temper to rival the largest beast had found a way to rein it in. For her he had squashed it. Samantha had been right.

"There's nothing noble about me." He glanced away. "If you don't mind, I'd like to be alone now."

"That's unfortunate because I am not going anywhere." She leaned down until there was almost no distance between them. All she had to do was lower her lips slightly and they'd brush against his cheek. "What if I were to tell you that you're the gentleman I most desire. What would you do then?" She pressed her lips against his cheek.

He groaned but she didn't think it was from pain. He wrapped his arms around her waist and pulled her fully against him. She laid atop him and could feel every inch of his delectable body. Kaitlin recalled how wonderful he'd felt in the pond. He'd been naked then, and now he was fully clothed, but she could still make out the details. They were burned in her memory, after all.

"Are you sure about this?" he asked. His voice was husky. "Because if I kiss you again, I'm never letting you go."

She didn't answer him with words. Kaitlin lowered her head and pressed her lips against his. He took over from there and ravaged her mouth with his. The kiss seemed to go on forever, and she felt truly plundered. He lifted his lips from hers and began to trail kisses down her cheek then to her neck.

Her body heated from his touch. There wasn't anywhere he hadn't explored with his hands and mouth. At least, what he could manage fully clothed and without moving from their current position.

"What are you doing to my sister?"

Kaitlin groaned and attempted to move. He held her firmly in place. "Your sister has agreed to marry me, and we're celebrating," he told her brother.

Her heart beat rapidly inside her chest with the beats thundering in her ears, and for a moment, the entire world disappeared around her. Nothing existed but her and the man she loved. Then everything came crashing down around her, and she was reminded they were not alone. Her brother was in the room, and she had to remain as calm as possible. She never dreamed she'd have the pleasure of being the Earl of Shelby's wife. It hadn't seemed possible, and it was difficult to accept it might be real.

To hear him state plainly he intended to marry her... That was as surreal as it could get. Of course, she couldn't allow him to act so high handed. She deserved to be asked, and she fully intended to remind him of that at the first opportunity. She glanced at her brother and smiled at him. She didn't know what else to do.

"Is that so?" Collin asked in a challenging tone. She adored her little brother and wanted to hug him tight. She'd refrain from doing so though. Kaitlin didn't want to embarrass him. "Then shouldn't you be speaking to me and asking for permission?"

Kaitlin grinned. Technically, Uncle Charles was who Shelby had to talk to, but she wouldn't correct Collin. Her brother wanted to protect her, it seemed, and she'd allow it. "Well?" She lifted a brow. "Considering you never once asked me or told me how you feel, the least you can do is explain it to my brother."

"I warned you," he said. "I told you I wasn't letting you go. You had your chance to run, and you decided to stay."

So that had been his proposal? She chuckled. Kaitlin didn't know why she'd expected anything less from him. "Lord Shelby would be happy to sit down and speak with you." She attempted to roll away again, but he wasn't letting her go.

"Gregory," he said. "I think we're past formalities."

He wanted her to use his given name. If she'd doubted the genuineness to his proposal, that inspired her more than him saying he loved her would. Not that she wouldn't love to hear those words from him, but she understood him better now. He was an extremely private person. "I love you too," she said softly.

He groaned. "Don't say that now. I love you. I do, but I have to go have a conversation with your brother and then track down Coventry. I don't want to wait too long to marry you. You will marry me, right?"

She kissed him softly. "I will. Now let me go so you can do all of that. Once we're married, we will have the rest of our life to be together, but first we have to make it happen."

He held her close and whispered in her ear. "I'm afraid. I don't know what I'd do if I lost you, but to never have you seems a far worse way to live."

Her heart hurt for him. Losing his mother had affected him far more than she'd thought. Samantha had tried to explain it to her, but she didn't fully grasp it until this moment. "We'll love each other every day no matter how long that might be." She brushed her hand over the uninjured part of his face. "And it will be perfect because we will be together."

He let her go and she rolled off of him then stood up. She nodded toward her brother. "Don't make it too difficult for him. He's had a rough day."

Collin grinned. "I'll keep that under advisement. I heard you already beat some sense into him with a cricket bat and a ball. I didn't realize you had to go to such extremes to secure a husband."

"You, dear brother, are a termagant." She grinned and left him alone with her fiancé. Soon she'd be Lady Shelby and have the right to kiss him whenever she wanted, and she fully intended to do so as often as possible. Kaitlin would also tell him she loved him several times a day. Maybe, if she said it enough, he'd believe it and let loose that fear he held inside of him. Her Gregory wasn't flawless, but he was the perfect gentleman for her. She couldn't wait to see where their lives together took them. There wasn't a doubt in her mind that it would be quite the adventure... After all, high society now had an earl that was a little less scandalous amongst its ranks. She couldn't expect him to reform completely. There were certain aspects of him that she wouldn't want to change for anything. The Earl of Shelby had fallen in love with her, and she intended to enjoy every second of being his wife.

EPILOGUE

*I*t was a bright and sunny day. A good day for outdoor activities, and the games Marian had planned were going well. Kaitlin stood on the far side of the lawn and watched as the men played a rousing game of cricket. They were quite... competitive. She'd never have believed they would all turn into savages over a game. If her fiancé were not playing, she might have stayed inside. Her foray into the game had made her realize she didn't like it much. She hated that she'd hurt him.

She was still getting accustomed to considering the Earl of Shelby as hers. Kaitlin loved him so much she nearly burst with the joy.

"Look at that smile on her face," Marian said and nudged Samantha. "I do believe she's in love."

"I hope so," Samantha replied with an amused tone. "Otherwise, I wouldn't understand why she agreed to marry my brother. He's an arse on a good day. Only someone in love would deign to take him on for the rest of their life."

Their teasing should bother her, but she refused to be upset. The old Kaitlin, the one that had shuttered at anything that brought her anxiety, would already be cringing. "Laugh all you want. I'm happy, and nothing is going to ruin that for me."

"Good for you," Marian said encouragingly. "There is no greater feeling than love. I'm glad I found Jonas, but if I hadn't, I suppose I wouldn't know what I was missing."

"I never thought..." Kaitlin swallowed hard. "It doesn't matter what I thought. Clearly, I was wrong. Love is a gift, and I am glad you have it with Jonas." She placed her hand on Marian's arm, then turned to Samantha. "And I hope one day you find someone to love as well. Someone that is brave enough to stand by your side and fight for you. We both know whoever this mythical man is will need to have the tenacity to stand up to your brother. He's quite overprotective of you."

She wasn't sure what had driven Gregory to push every man interested in Samantha out of her life, but she did know he loved his sister. It was his deluded way of protecting her. When she had the chance, she'd have a little talk with him and how he treated Samantha. She deserved to find love, and Kaitlin intended to assist her in finding it.

"My brother believes he knows what is best for me," Samantha began. "But he's wrong. He doesn't know what I really want and never has. He's never bothered to take the time to actually ask me if any of the men he challenged interested me."

"Don't worry," Kaitlin said in an attempt to reassure her. "I'll do my best to distract him and prevent him from any future mistakes." She grinned. "He'll be too busy making me happy to make you miserable."

"I wish you luck with that." Samantha's lips twitched. "You're going to need all the fortitude you have to deal with him every day. I commend you for wanting to take on the challenge."

In Kaitlin's mind, Gregory was worth it. She turned her attention back toward the game. It appeared to be wrapping up. Gregory was standing near a wicket with a bat in hand. Lord Harrington held the leather-bound ball and prepared to pitch it. He wound his hand up and the ball flew. Gregory hit it, and it went past all the fielders and his team erupted in cheers. She assumed that meant they won, but she hadn't paid much attention. Even if she had, she knew very little about the game and couldn't tell one way or the other. Her lessons hadn't gone as far as all the rules of the game. Lord Asthey had only concentrated on teaching her how to hit the ball.

Gregory tossed his bat to the ground and then turned to glance her way. He jogged over to her side and pulled her into his arms, swinging her around. "We won," he said.

"I guessed as much," she said. "What does this mean?"

He kissed her and then set her down. "It means Darcy and I won the bet."

"I realize that," she said. "But I don't know what winning the bet gains you."

"The right to brag?"

"That sounded more like a question than an answer."

"She's not wrong," Samantha said. "I have to agree with Kaitlin on this one, brother mine. What exactly are the four of you up to?" She gestured toward Lord Harrington, Lord Darcy, and Lord Asthey, then glanced back at the Earl of Shelby.

"I'm afraid that will have to remain between us,"

her brother said. "Let's just say Harrington and Asthey won't be happy they lost."

Kaitlin hated not knowing. She wanted to press the issue but decided against it. Chances were she would have better luck obtaining the information from him in private.

She placed her hand on his arm. "Come walk with me."

"Gladly," he agreed.

They walked away from the crowd and headed toward the gardens. He pulled her close once they were out of view from everyone and lowered his head until his lips were pressed against hers. The kiss deepened and she moaned in pleasure. Kaitlin doubted she'd ever get used to the feelings he invoked within her.

He ended the kiss and lifted his head to fully meet her gaze. "I love you."

"I know," she said.

He lifted a brow. "Do you now?"

She giggled a little at his mocking tone. "I do," she answered. "Otherwise, I never would have agreed to marry you. Now kiss me again before someone decides to interrupt us."

"Happily," he said and proceeded to kiss her. She

couldn't wait until they were married. Kissing Gregory was one of life's greatest pleasures, and she fully intended to enjoy it as much as possible for the rest of her life.

EXCERPT: CONFESSIONS OF A HELLION

BLUESTOCKINGS DEFYING ROGUES
BOOK SEVEN

DAWN BROWER

USA TODAY
BESTSELLING AUTHOR

Dawn Brower

Confessions
of a Hellion

Weston Manor, 1823

They entered the ballroom. It was already filled to capacity. Even if they remained wallflowers, they'd be unable to avoid all the guests. Everyone must have accepted the invite. The Duke and Duchess of Weston didn't entertain often, and they were all probably curious. Lady Samantha couldn't blame them. She had been rather intrigued herself. She loved balls and dancing. Being invited to one of the exclusive country events at the end of the season thrilled her. She scanned the room for the duchess and found her on the far edge of the dance floor.

Marian only cared about one thing. Securing the

Duchess of Weston's assistance in learning to be a doctor. She glanced around the room until she located her, then turned to Samantha and Kaitlin. "If you'll excuse me," she said to them. "I'm going to talk to the duchess."

"Don't forget to ask her this time," Samantha said. "I see Lord Darcy; I'm heading in his direction." She didn't really want the Earl of Darcy's attention, but it sounded good to say she wanted to dance with him. "I'd hate for him to not be able to locate me. Come with me, Katie, so I'm not standing alone."

"So you can leave me stranded as you run off with him?" Kaitlin grumbled under her breath. "You'll owe me for this."

"Don't worry, dear," Samantha replied as she dragged Kaitlin with her. "I'll find you a dance partner too. Isn't that Lord Asthey talking to Lord Darcy?" Her heart thundered in her chest. While she hadn't really wanted to see Lord Darcy, she did want to see Lord Asthey. He was so handsome. Both Lord Darcy and Lord Asthey were blond, had gorgeous blue eyes, and amazing physiques. Judging them by looks alone wasn't enough though. Only one of them made her heart race and filled her with excitement. The problem of course was he didn't notice her as anything more than his friend's little sister.

Kaitlin sighed and let Samantha lead her to the two earls. "I don't need to dance." She shook her head vigorously. "I can find a book to read and sit in the corner."

Samantha stopped and stared at her friend. "You will do no such thing." How could Kaitlin not want to dance? "Do you not like Lord Asthey?" That seemed even worse somehow. Samantha adored him. She wanted him for herself, but gave up on that notion a while ago. If she couldn't get pleasure from dancing with him perhaps her friend could. Not that she wanted Lord Asthey to fall in love with Kaitlin, but he seemed to like her. Samantha wasn't so selfish as to not wish her friend happiness. Even if it felt as if she were being stabbed in the heart every time Lord Asthey smiled fondly at Kaitlin... She shook that pain away and pasted a smile on her face.

"Lord Asthey is likeable enough," Kaitlin said in a good-natured tone. "But I don't like dancing." She wrinkled her nose in disgust.

"Nonsense," Samantha said and waved her hand. "You just haven't found the right partner yet."

She narrowed her gaze. Was that her brother lounging in the corner? Samantha blew out a breath. She'd have to be careful. If Gregory, Lord Shelby, her overprotective brother thought she was getting too attached to the Earl of Darcy he might act rashly. In her brother's mind no one was good enough for her. Especially one of the wicked earls, as they dubbed themselves. Unfortunately, Lord Asthey was also in that particular group. Shelby adored his friends. He just didn't want any of his friends to pay any attention to his little sister.

Kaitlin placed her hand on Samantha's arm. "I really do not wish to dance."

What was she supposed to do? Kaitlin would be more comfortable hiding in a corner. She had to help her friend break out of her shell in some way. If she insisted on gluing herself to a wall she'd never find love. Kaitlin deserved to find someone that would adore her. Samantha wanted to help guide her there. If she couldn't have the one man she loved, then at least Kaitlin would. "One dance," Samantha said. "After that we can leave the ballroom if you wish."

Kaitlin's shoulders drooped. She closed her eyes and took a deep breath. "Fine," she said. "I'll dance one but after that I don't want you to pressure me into anything else I don't wish to do. I'll have your word on it." She glared at Samantha.

"I promise," Samantha said earnestly and crossed her finger over her heart. "You may rely upon it."

She looped her arm through Kaitlin's and led her the rest of the way to Lord Darcy and Lord Asthey. They were deep in conversation when they arrived next to them.

"I guess we are co-captains at this year's cricket match," Darcy said. "We have more options for teammates here. What should we ask for as our prize when we win?"

"A little arrogant of you to count our winnings before they're earned, isn't it?" Asthey lifted a brow. "Shelby is damn good at the game. I should know."

They both stopped talking when they arrived. "We're not interrupting are we?" Samantha batted her eyelashes at them. She was well aware of their yearly cricket match. Whenever she could she'd sneak out to watch some of their private matches. Not all of them took place at country parties. One thing stayed true throughout the years. They all played and the four of them divided up differently each year. That was how they kept things between them fair.

Kaitlin had a far away expression on her face. Her friend was probably daydreaming about something she wouldn't share. Samantha doubted she had heard anything the two earls had been discussing. Sometimes Kaitlin lived in a world of her own.

Samantha wished she could lose herself in her own mind every now and then. She had too many plans to live in a make-believe world. Samantha glanced at her friend then at the two earls. "Are you going to dance this evening?" Perhaps a little blunt but Samantha wasn't known for her shy and demure demeanor. Her brother often called her a hellion. She wouldn't apologize for who she was for any reason.

"I…" Asthey stumbled over the words.

"Why of course," Darcy said smoothly. He bowed. "Would you care to dace Lady Samantha?"

Why couldn't Asthey have asked her to dance? He had started to speak first. Would he have actually asked if Darcy hadn't interrupted him? Somehow she doubted it. "That would be lovely," she answered him. She managed to keep a bright smile on her face even though she didn't feel anything resembling excitement. She held out her hand to him and he led her to the floor. At least it wasn't a waltz. She didn't want to dance such an intimate set with Lord Darcy.

Asthey bowed to Kaitlin and said something to her. She shook her head vigorously. Did her friend just decline to dance with him? Samantha seethed inwardly. Kaitlin had the one thing Samantha coveted before her and she had said no. That was…

wrong. She turned to Darcy as he led her through the dance. They didn't talk much and for that she was thankful. Asthey and Kaitlin strolled around the room. Samantha was green with jealousy but she tamped it down.

"Are you enjoying the ball?" Lord Darcy asked.

"Of course," she answered smoothly. "Are you?"

"Yes," he said. "It's been quite entertaining."

This had to be the most mundane conversation she'd ever had. Through it all she kept the smile on her face. She also kept track of every step Lord Asthey and Kaitlin took. They seemed to be having an animated conversation. Whatever Lord Asthey was saying Kaitlin found riveting. She wished she could hear it. Hell, Samantha just wished she could hold Lord Asthey's attention as long as Kaitlin seemed to be holding it.

Would he court her? Dance with her? Love her? Would Samantha wake one day to find an engagement announcement in the Times? Her heart broke at the thought. How was she to survive in a world where one of her best friends married the man she loved? What was wrong with her? She had to let him go. He clearly didn't see her the same way. She turned her attention to Darcy. He at least looked at her as an attractive female. He might not love her, but he appreciated her.

The dance came to an end and Lord Darcy led her to the edge of the dance floor. He bowed and said, "Thank you for the dance."

"It was my pleasure, Lord Darcy." Where were Kaitlin and Asthey? She had lost track of them at the end of the dance.

"If you'll excuse me I see Lord Harrington. There is something I must discuss with him."

Samantha wasn't a fool. He would want to discuss their upcoming cricket match. She might try to eavesdrop later. Samantha didn't want to miss the pertinent details. She wanted to be able to watch and secretly cheer for Lord Asthey, but she could gather that information later. It was far more important to locate Kaitlin and Lord Asthey. She curtsied. "Until next time."

His lips twitched. "I look forward to it." With those words he left her alone and headed toward Lord Harrington.

At that moment she caught a glimpse of Kaitlin out of the corner of her eye. She was alone. Where had Asthey gone? Samantha scanned the room feverishly. He'd disappeared. She lost her chance at securing a dance with him. The strands of a waltz filled the room. She turned to leave the ballroom before anyone noticed the crestfallen expression on her face. She ran right into a male. He had a hard muscular chest that most women might find appealing. Samantha glanced up and met Lord Asthey's gaze.

"My apologies," he said. "I should have been paying attention better." He glanced past her to the other side of the room. He'd been heading toward Harrington too. She'd let him go plan with his friends but this was the only chance she had with him. Samantha wanted one dance. Just one. Was that too much to ask?

"You can make it up to me by dancing with me." She smiled softly, silently begging him. "Please." It was the waltz. She wanted to feel his arms around her. So she could pretend for a few brief moments he loved her.

"I..." He swallowed hard. "Of course." Lord Asthey held out his hand to her and led her to the floor.

Samantha felt as if she were floating on clouds. Lord Asthey was a marvelous dancer and led her expertly around the floor. This was a dream. One she had every night but until now hadn't experienced in reality. Of course it wasn't exactly as she had dreamed it. In her fantasies he confessed his love and asked her to marry him. A lady couldn't have everything could she?

She would remember this dance for the rest of her life. It probably would be the only dance she had with him. If this were all she would have she'd cherish it. When she was old and alone she could look back on it with fondness. If she were brave enough she'd confess her feelings. Even hellions had trouble spilling all their secrets though. Some confessions wouldn't unburden the soul. It was best she kept her deepest desires to herself. She wouldn't want to scare Lord Asthey away. It would break her heart even more if she never saw him again.

The dance came to an end and he led her off the floor. They hadn't said a word throughout the entire dance. That was all right with her. It was enough to have had this one dance. She smiled at him hoping he could see how much she cared. He didn't. He bowed and made his excuses. It was over before it ever had a chance to begin. Lord Asthey left her alone and went toward his friends. Samantha's smile wobbled a little. She had to leave before the world became privy to her anguish. Without saying a word she turned on her heels and exited the ballroom. Kaitlin could take care of herself. Marian was still there after all... Samantha barely contained her tears until she reached her chambers. Once there she let go and cried all her pain out.

When she had no more tears to shed she sat up and wiped her face. There. That was done. Now she could move on and find a man who would love her. Lord Asthey didn't know what he was missing.

If only she could make herself believe that...

EXCERPT: CHANCE OF LOVE

SCANDAL MEETS LOVE 6

DAWN BROWER

Scandal Meets Love
Chance of Love
USA TODAY BESTSELLING AUTHOR
Dawn Brower

PROLOGUE

April 1816

Spring had always been her favorite season. Lady Lenora St. Martin didn't have much else to look forward to and the very idea of new beginnings appealed to her. Every spring new life sprouted and the barren landscape was filled with beauty and wonder. That also applied to the London ballrooms. New debutantes were launched in society and the latest crop of true English beauties was put on display for those gentlemen in search of a wife.

Lenora had never been considered a beauty…

She'd accepted her lot in life a long time ago. She

DAWN BROWER

had dark brown hair and hazel eyes, both boring. Her attributes along with her shyness kept her position as a wallflower secure. No one noticed her and most of the time that was all right with her. A crowded ballroom tended to bring out her worst anxieties. Her cousin Bennett, the Marquess of Holton, insisted she attend social gatherings. Lenora understood his reasons even if she didn't particularly agree with them. Bennett hoped she'd find a suitor, fall in love, and then marry so she could have a family of her own. All of those things sounded wonderful. None of them were likely to happen. At least not with her...

This ball, the one most debutantes and their mothers clamored to attend, was a good example. The young misses were all flirting with their gentlemen suitors and their mothers gossiped with other matrons. The wallflowers did what they did best—hugged the walls. Lenora; on the other hand, did none of that. She didn't merely stand by the wall hoping some wayward gentleman would discover her and lead her to the dance floor. That would have been too simple and probably preferred by her cousin. No, Lenora didn't do anything by normal standards. She hated to be noticed and would have loved to have remained at home reading one of her favorite novels. So she attempted to make the best of a terrible situation and hid in the darkest most obscure corner she could find.

Spring might mean new beginnings, but it also meant new social gatherings. It led to her greatest discomfort and she dreaded it. If she'd been left alone to walk in the gardens or bask in the warmth of sunlight streaming through her bedroom window she'd have been gloriously happy. Instead she was forced into ballrooms and hiding in corners.

"What's a lovely woman such as yourself doing in this dark corner?" His voice was as warm as honey on a hot summer day. It's tempting sweetness washed over her and made her crave a taste...of something. He was also the biggest rake in all of London. Julian Everleigh, the Duke of Ashley was a notorious seducer. "Come dance with me little mouse."

Lenora wrinkled her nose at his endearment for her. She adored Julian, but she knew better than to accept anything he offered. He visited her cousin often enough she should be unaffected by his flirtations. They thrilled her though and she wanted to savor them whenever he deigned to speak to her. "No thank you," she said softly. "I'm all right, promise."

He chuckled lightly and then tilted his lips upward into the most sinful smile she'd ever witnessed. Not that she'd seen many… Most gentlemen failed to notice her let alone smile purposely in her direction. "You shouldn't promise something that isn't true little one," he said. "I don't ever bother with a promise because I know myself too well. I'll break them the first chance presented to me." Julian winked at her and it sent flutters through her stomach she'd never felt before in her entire life. "Instead I'll ensure you will never forget dancing with me. I'm quite good at it." He held out his hand. "Now please, do me the honor of spending a few moments with me. I'm in desperate need of protection from unwanted advances." He leaned down just enough so that she could feel his warm breath when he spoke. "Are you willing to be my savior?"

In that moment she'd have promised him anything, but she held back. He said promises were nothing to him. The duke openly admitted to breaking them often. The vow she was about to make would be empty words to him. So instead she smiled, even if it was a little wobbly. Dancing in front of everyone terrified her. "I can try…"

"That's all anyone can ask," he told her.

Why did he have to be so gorgeous? He was too handsome and way too pretty to be paying any attention to her. His golden blond hair rivaled the sun in brilliance and his blue eyes were more dazzling than the most exquisite sapphire. She could easily become lost in his charming veneer if she allowed herself to be. "I supp..suppose," she stuttered over the word. Lenora cleared her throat and began again. "I suppose that is true."

"So?" He lifted a brow. "Will you join me for the next set?"

She nodded as the strands of a waltz filled the room. Lenora almost groaned when she realized what she'd agreed to. The waltz was the most intimate dances and she'd never danced one with a male other than her cousin. Heck, she'd never danced at all with a male besides her cousin... That didn't detract from her dilemma. A waltz with the duke would cause a stir and she'd be so close to him... Her hand shook as she placed it in his. "Lead the way, Your Grace."

He led her to the floor and then he twirled her into the dance before she had time to change her mind, and she'd been close to doing so. The closer she'd stepped toward the light and the prying gazes of the ton she'd become increasingly more anxious. He'd been wise to take the decision away from her.

Julian was an amazing dancer, but that shouldn't have surprised her. Everything about him or that he did seemed to be perfect. "Now," he began. "This doesn't seem so bad does it, little one?"

At least he hadn't called her a mouse again… "No," she agreed. It was actually quite exhilarating. Lenora felt as if she was floating on air.

"I've always considered dancing to be too decadent to be done properly in a public forum," he began. "At least the sort I prefer."

She pushed her eyebrows together. "I'm not sure I follow…"

"I wouldn't expect you would," he replied secretively. "One day you might understand. Perhaps you'll tell me when you do." The corner of his lip turned upward almost…arrogantly. As if only he really understood the secrets of the world…

"I suspect, Your Grace, that our paths won't cross much in the coming years." The duke might be one of her cousin's friends, but she fully expected, at some juncture, to live on her own. Once she reached her majoring in a few months she planned to travel. Maybe to Italy… She hadn't fully decided yet. "We don't keep the same company and in time the little connections we have will dissipate."

"Perhaps," he agreed. "Time will tell I suppose." He twirled her around the floor expertly.

Lenora wouldn't ever forget this moment. She would unlikely never dance again, at least not like this. She was grateful she'd allowed the duke to convince her to participate. Afterward she'd likely find her way to her favorite corner to hide. In her darkest moments she'd be able to travel back to this waltz and recall it, and Julian fondly. If she believed she had a chance of something more with him... She shook that thought away. Loving him was a terrible idea and perhaps the only thing she regretted. This was a kindness, while out of character for him, but she shouldn't expect anything else from him.

The strands of the waltz ended and disappointment filled her. She'd tried to brush his request off at the start and now she never wanted the dance to end. The duke twirled her one last time around the floor and then led her to where their dance had begun. He bowed and kissed her gloved hand. "Thank you for your benevolence, my lady." His blue eyes twinkled with mischief. "And for being my protector when I need it."

She should be thanking him. He had awakened

feelings in her she'd believed long buried. Her heart burst with happiness and affection for this man. "You don't require my protection any more than you needed to dance with me." She frowned. Lenora still couldn't discern his motives for insisting on leading her in the waltz. "Either way the dance was lovely. I'm grateful I didn't insist against it."

He laughed lightly and shook his head. "Little mouse you're always so formal." Julian bowed again. "The pleasure was all mine." He glanced over his shoulder and then back at her. "Pardon me," he said. "I must attend to something important." His smile was bright and appeared genuine. "Enjoy the rest of your evening, my lady." With those words he spun on his heels and headed in the opposite direction.

Lenora smiled as she watched him wander off. She was starting to believe she had misjudged him. He'd been charming, as expected, but also kind and generous with his time. The duke hadn't been required to dance with her. No gentleman was. That made his attention all the more precious to her.

She wandered away from her favorite corner for willingly the first time all evening. Earlier didn't count because Julian had to coax her away from it. Perhaps she should leave the ballroom and explore the gardens. It was starting to become suffocating in the ballroom. Lenora's happiness was nearly bursting from within her. She hugged herself and twirled around as she made her way down the empty hallway leading to the balcony. There was a small staircase on the balcony that led down to the gardens.

Voices echoed back to her. Two male voices to be more precise and both were recognizable.

"Did she dance?" Her cousin asked. Why was Bennett so concerned about her dancing? Why couldn't he leave her to make her own decisions?

"Of course she did," Julian responded. "Do you doubt my ability to charm a woman?" He sounded so...disgusted. Was that because he had to dance with Lenora or because Bennett had doubted his ability? "I can coax any woman to do, well, anything," he boasted. "But a wallflower? That's not even a challenge."

She'd been jubilant until that moment. Now every amount of joy she'd held inside of her deflated in an instant. He'd appeared so kind earlier... How had she gotten it so wrong?

"Attention from you should have caught the notice of all the eligible gentleman in the room," Bennett said. "They'll want to know why the Duke of

Ashley bothered with a wallflower. Soon she'll have more callers than she wants."

She didn't want any callers… A part of her hated her cousin for insinuating himself into her life this way. Why did he ask his friend to pay attention to her? Did he hate having her live with him that much? She'd thought they were closer than that…

"I've done you this favor," the duke said. "Don't ask it of me ever again." His tone was harsh and unyielding. It stabbed her in her fragile heart. She'd been on the brink of falling in love with him. The Duke of Ashley didn't deserve her affection. Lenora doubted he was worthy of any woman's love.

Tears stung her eyes and slid down her cheek. She brushed them away with a swipe of her fingertips. They wouldn't help her and they were as useless as her ability to read people. Lenora hardened her heart in that moment. She'd never play the fool again. It was time she learned to weave her way through society without letting another touch her soul again. She'd never be so easily duped again, but she had a lot to learn. There was one person who could teach her and she'd do whatever it took to convince her. That one person was the new Lulia Prescott—the gypsy Duchess of Clare…

With her decision made she rushed out of the

ballroom and walked all the way to the Holton townhouse. She'd need a good night of rest before she started her journey. Her first stop would be Tenby, Wales to visit with the duchess. After that she'd travel as planned. When she returned to London again she'd be an entirely different, better woman.

AFTERWORD

Thank you so much for taking the time to read my book.

Your opinion matters!

Please take a moment to review this book on your favorite review site and share your opinion with fellow readers.

www.authordawnbrower.com

ABOUT THE AUTHOR

USA TODAY Bestselling author, DAWN BROWER writes both historical and contemporary romance. There are always stories inside her head; she just never thought she could make them come to life. That creativity has finally found an outlet.

Growing up she was the only girl out of six children. She is a single mother of two teenage boys; there is never a dull moment in her life. Reading books is her favorite hobby and she loves all genres.

BB bookbub.com/authors/dawn-brower

f facebook.com/1DawnBrower

🐦 twitter.com/1DawnBrower

📷 instagram.com/1DawnBrower

g goodreads.com/dawnbrower

Scheming with My Duke

Secluded with My Hellion

Heart's Intent

One Heart to Give

Unveiled Hearts

Heart of the Moment

Kiss My Heart Goodbye

Heart in Waiting

Broken Curses

The Enchanted Princess

The Bespelled Knight

The Magical Hunt

Ever Beloved

Forever My Earl

Always My Viscount

Infinitely My Marquess

EternallyMyDuke

Kismet Bay

Once Upon a Christmas

New Year Revelation

All Things Valentine

Luck At First Sight

Endless Summer Days

Coming Soon

A Witch's Charm

All Out of Gratitude

Christmas Ever After

www.ingramcontent.com/pod-product-compliance
Lightning Source LLC
Chambersburg PA
CBHW022121170626
46808CB00002B/801